RANXUS

Wingblade Unleashed

PENDRAGON

notionpress.com

INDIA • SINGAPORE • MALAYSIA

ISBN
Paperback 979-8-89699-380-3
Hardcase 979-8-89744-268-3

CONTENTS

Chapter – 1

XERKERS

Lying on top of the white grass was a 10-year-old boy. As he stared at the various coloured energies that was floating around in every direction, all of them converging at a semicircular shaped domelike structure made of silver and gold energies that seemed to be the core of the planet he was on. Not far from where the boy lay was a kingdom full of beings hustling around. As he kept staring at the energy and stretched out his hand into the midst of the energy layer, a flash of lightning brightened up the sky.

Next moment, the sky turned dark and 6 blood skulls shaped in circular form appeared in various places in the sky. Blood started raining down on the white grass turning it red. Another flash of lightning and the boy was standing in the middle of the room horrified by the sight he saw. It was a big room and everything was ransacked and furniture destroyed. There were sounds of blades and voices and body pieces and bloodstains covering the whole room like a river.

The boy started crying out loud. He called for his parents and unknown figures appeared before him and spoke:

"The Wingblade must fall."

They all said it in one voice which scared the boy as he continued to cry. The figures smiled and enclosed their hands into a pentagon shape and with a flash of light, the boy's body was pierced with hexagonal shaped rods with the colour of space. There was a sudden scream. The next moment a shiny light flashed in front of him and a voice echoed saying:

"Leo, the end is coming. Reach out to me and save everything before you lose them."

15-year-old Leo woke up, drenched in sweat. He took a cloth which was lying on the bed beside him and wiped his face. He got up and jumped down from his bed which hung in mid-air with the help of two arc shaped triangle which were horizontally joined to both edges of the bed. In the middle of the triangle was a small white crystallized ball which kept spinning. As soon as Leo jumped down the bed, the ball stopped spinning and the triangle retracted into a single line which in turn retracted the bed into a rod that lay on the ground.

There was a movement on his left side. A circular ring with a semi-transparent ray of white and red-orangish light in the ceiling emitted a bright white light. Underneath the ring, pure glass pieces fell onto the floor and disappeared automatically as soon as they touched the ground into nothing. The glass pieces fell, emitting that white light. It was an amazing sight.

The whole room lit up, and the entrance of a rectangular window spiralled away into arc-shaped cones, which slid into the frame attached to it. The view outside of the window was always the same at which Leo used to stare when he got up. The vast sea sparkled like in the sunlight, chirping of birds in the distance and the cool breeze that entered the room from beyond what looked like a barrier.

There wasn't any furniture except four rods that lay in the other corner. His clothes were sweaty. He just stood up and stared at the view outside his window, as usual, pondering over the dream he saw. After a pause, he walked to a smaller room, which had no door; instead, a symbol in the shape of blades in a two-sided way with a trapezium-shaped cross symbol in the center, called nexus, was at the doorstep. As soon as he stepped on the symbol of nexus, the blades again split apart and circled around him, making his clothes disappear. As he entered the bathroom, a door appeared in the shape of the nexus.

There were three circular shaped pits filled with water at the mid-corners on the three sides of the room. A mirror was suspended into the air in front of him. He walked towards the center, and as he was nearing the center of the room, the water suddenly turned blood red and rose towards the mirror and splashed against it with a huge force which almost broke it. Writing in blood appeared which read:

"The Wingblade must fall."

He was scared and closed his eyes. When he opened it again, it was gone. He froze where he was standing. After a while, he found the courage and walked and reached the center. The water, which had gone back to its original state as if nothing had happened, rose again and engulfed him in the form of a cyclone.

Hands made of water came out of the cyclone and washed him and brushed his teeth. He refreshed quickly and walked back towards the door as the water again went back to its original state. As he reached near the door, the door disappeared, and he stepped on the symbol again, which made a new set of clothes appear on his body.

He walked out of the bathroom into the kitchen, where his sister was preparing breakfast. Everything in the kitchen was hanging in mid-air and had same arc shaped triangles at the edges of the kitchen wares and all the furniture in the kitchen. His sister sensed his presence and spoke:

"Leo, come, sit down at the table. It's almost done."

She turned around and came towards the table, which hung in mid-air too. She sat down at the table after placing the breakfast for them to eat. She had eyes with a shade of purple, her hair tied into a single plait with a shade of violet and black and her lips as sweet looking as strawberry. She was wearing a t-shirt and jeans, and on top of the t-shirt lay an apron. Leo looked at her spoke:

Leo: "Sis Kate, It's delicious."

Kate: "Hahaha. Thank you, Leo. Have you readied your things to go to school? I am sorry, Leo. Today, I won't be accompanying you to school as I have to go to work early. (Looking at the sad face of Leo, Kate spoke:) Don't be sad. I will be picking you up after school."

Kate hurriedly ate her breakfast and got up. After placing the dishes in the sink. The plates then got sucked into the hole in the middle of the sink and washing noises came from inside the hole. She quickly came near Leo and kissed his forehead before she left. Leo also finished his breakfast soon and went back to his room. As soon as he entered the room, he just touched the rod which was on the ground from which he had walked away to the bathroom earlier with his hand and it popped back up into his bed. He pulled out a drawer which was attached onto his bed and took out the spectacle and wore it on his eyes.

The spectacle had features of a smart device which consisted of a phone, T.V., etc. At the end of the spectacle's frame, which was resting near the ear, there was a tiny circular sensor attached that could read the brain waves. In short, it could access what the user was thinking and wanted to do and, if needed, execute it for him/her. He just thought of watching T.V., and the sensor sensed it and opened it on a widescreen automatically.

An old movie was going on, which was his favourite. For quite a while, he just watched it silently, and just as a big climax was about to happen, a sudden call interrupted him. He just smiled at the name Jay which flashed in front of his spectacles with few options like take call, etc., at the corner of his spectacles where his name flashed. He just thought of picking up the call, and the spectacles just sensed his thoughts and automatically picked up the call.

Jay: "Yo, dude. What's the holdup? You are late. I am already at the station. Get here already."

Leo: "Yo. Sorry, sorry, I didn't realize the time. I will be there in a jiffy. Wait for me at the station. Seeya."

Jay: "Seeya."

Leo hurriedly got up and ran towards the door wearing the spectacles. As he neared the door, he just stepped onto the doorstep and passed right through the door, onto the porch. A bright light fell upon the view in front of him. He was standing in a closed-form of semi-circular lift shaped cabin with a glass wall in a semi-circular shape with a door behind him. He was standing right on top of the nexus symbol. There were buildings nearby his own.

The building was vertically rectangle shaped. His building and a few other buildings were connected in a circular shape to a central pipeline. The pipeline was connected to a container at the bottom which was further connected to a teleportation device. As soon as he stepped on nexus, the blades split apart into two and circled around his feet, and he just disappeared.

Next moment he reappeared at a station. The station was horizontally arc shaped. On the platform, many people were waiting for the train to arrive. At the edge of the platform were vertical arc- shaped rods that had holes in them. Just attached to the rods were transparent gates made of water. Just as Leo reappeared at the station, he accidentally bumped into a girl. Though it was a slight brush, the girl glared at him as if he had smacked her head. Leo apologized and hurried to where his friend was.

He came to a standstill and was trying to catch his breath when he felt a tap on his shoulder. A young boy who seemed to be of the same age as Leo. It was none another than Jay, Leo's friend.

Leo: "Hey, buddy. What's up?"

Jay: "What's up? Hahaha. You almost missed the train to school. Well, no worries now, since, you reached in the nick of time. The train's almost here."

Leo just smiled at Jay, and they went on talking about stuff. The station was, as usual crowded. There were seats placed in front of transparent glass walls. The iron rods on the rails were full of small holes from which a small circular pipe was protruding upward. Suddenly there was a yank behind Leo, and the train slowly entered the station.

The train had no wheels. Instead, it had the same holes with a slanting semi-circular pipe connected at the bottom. The lower part of the train was made of iron, while the upper body was made fully of transparent glass. It stopped at the station, and as soon as the door opened, a sudden push made Leo and Jay rush along with the crowd into the train. The door shut, and the train started moving. It was solely moving on air that was absorbed through the pipes outside the barrier surrounding the city. The whole ceiling of the city was visible through the transparent glass.

Tall buildings with a ring of pipe attached circularly on top of those buildings was sight to behold. The train just moved so smoothly and fast that no one felt any jerk while moving. As the train neared its destination, there was a sudden explosion that shook the whole city and even the train. As Leo looked up, he saw the barrier was falling apart. The next moment there was a huge explosion at the destination of the train as it was slowing down at the station and making it suddenly stop in its tracks. Another explosion occurred in front of the coach that Leo was riding on. The doors swung open, and everyone just scrambled forward.

As the barrier fell apart, suddenly, drones flew in to the people who were divided into small groups, each group with a drone. The drones spew out nanomachines that made a transparent barrier around the groups to prevent the people from smelling harmful gases. Another explosion, and they were surrounded by thousands of unknown figures. As Leo's gaze turned towards the explosion, there were no buildings except burning rubbles. The unknown figures that surrounded them were dressed in clothing of dark purple colour with a symbol of circular arc-shaped arrow blades in silver colour. In front of their clothing, arc-shaped slits were extending from the chest to the abdomen on the left and right side. In the middle was a circular maze shaped structure from which arc-shaped blades were connected, shining bright silver.

Their eyes were narrow and of bright purple colour, same as of Leo's sister and instead of a nose, had long slit across on both of their cheeks which opened and closed like a fish's mouth. Each one had a symbol of hexagonal-shaped arc headed arrow blades tattooed on their faces. They were gazing with an intense fury at the group of people in the front. Leo was amongst that group. An unknown figure who appeared to be the leader among them stepped forward and stared in their direction. His eyes glared at the sight of Leo and muttered in a grunting voice:

"At last, he has been found."

The leader just raised his hand and pointed at the group, and all of his fellow mates just sprang at them with lightning speed. The group was frozen with fear. Suddenly there were attacks from behind the group.

Chapter – 2

RANXUS

A group of personnel dressed in a black and silver suit appeared. Each one had a holographic gun with a short silencer attached to the end. As one of the personnel pressed the trigger of the gun, the gun split into five separate drones, and they formed a pentagonal shape horizontally and shot solar bullets at the incoming enemies. But those shots didn't have any effect on them. The leader just slaughtered those personnel with a single wave of his hand. The next moment he just disappeared and reappeared in front of Leo and caught his hand and threw him out of the barrier.

As Leo was thrown by them, Jay couldn't muster up the courage to save him as he was frozen with fear. Leo fell right in the middle of the enemy's horde as they gazed upon him with an intense fury. They bared their eyes as each one wanted to tear him to pieces. Leo was shaking. The enemy leader just walked slowly towards him while speaking:

"This is the end of the road for you. Spill out where the piece of star rune is or I will have to torture it out of you."

Leo just stared at the leader, too scared to move or speak. As he reached near him and stretched out his hand to grab his neck, Jay suddenly got up and was about to run in to save him when petals with shades of white and blue engulfed Leo. A figure dressed in clothing of blue, white and orange shade was standing in front of him with the figure's back facing him. The clothing was in the shape similar to an armour. Although it didn't seem to be an armour completely, and it had a symbol of two arrow- headed blades on both sides of the nexus symbol coloured in blue, engraved on the backside of the figure vertically. The lower part of the figure was covered with pants made of wings with shades of orange and blue. Wings shaped blades were connected to the symbol on the back, which extended to the front which couldn't be seen.

The stranger sensed Leo's fear and turned towards him and spoke:

"Calm down. My name is Jin, and I'm a Cloudscar. The people you see in front of you are our enemies and are called Xerkers and sent here to kill you. But you don't have to worry because I'll protect you. "

Leo: "Ranxus? Cloudscar? Xerkers? I don't understand anything. (He spoke while trembling with fear.)."

Jin touched Leo's head and spoke again:

"I'll explain later. Right now, I need to take care of these guys. Calm down now. I'll keep you safe."

When Leo looked at Jin, he got scared a bit but slowly stopped trembling as Jin's voice was soothing enough to calm him down. Jin had six eyes, which were crisscrossed to each other with a shade of orange and white. He had no nose except nostrils which were vertically arced. There was a helically shaped wing with blades at the end tattooed across his nose and cheeks. In the front, there were tattooed blade-shaped openings in the form of ribs from which the wing-shaped blades were connected to the symbol on the back.

Just then, there was a sudden noise and as they both looked in the direction, they saw a group of Xerkers dashing towards them at high speed. Before even the group of Xerkers could move their hands, Jin quickly spun around, waving his right hand, and eight of two circular rings made of clouds, crisscrossed with each other at its diameter appeared around Jin in a circular formation. The pair of circular rings revolved around each other at its diameter, with a shining circular blade forming around the circumference of the rings. As if connected by chains to Jin's body, it flew towards the enemies with lightning speed. In an instant, the enemies disintegrated into pieces. The rest of the Xerkers glared at them and backed off a little, hesitating to attack. Just then, an unknown figure who appeared to be the leader among them stepped forward and spoke:

"Damn pathetic fools! You can't even capture these guys, huh! Why don't you two die right away? (Looking at Jin and Leo) which would make things easier for us."

Without another word, the leader just enclosed his hands in the form of a triangle, and a big star appeared in front of his hand from which arc-crone shaped blades sprung at them twisting in the air. There was a flash of light, and all arc-crones disappeared without a trace in the blink of an eye.

Three unknown figures were standing on top of some kind of air board which was in the same shape as the symbol at the back of Jin. They came down on the ground, and as soon as they stepped on the ground, the air board just split up in the middle and seeped into their shoes. All three unknown figures were wearing the same clothing and had the same features as Jin with different eye colours. Two of them were men, and the third was a girl so beautiful that words cannot say with her hair short and slanting sideways diagonally on her forehead. Her eyes were mesmerizing. She gave Leo a beautiful smile through her wet lips as she ran towards him to hug but Jin stopped her and told her to hold it until they were safe.

Leo was flustered due to the girl's behaviour just then. He kept stealing glances at her. Jin smirked a little at the sight of the three and spoke:

"Jeez! You are here at last. Man! What took you guys so long to reach here? I was tired of waiting. Here, hold on to Leo and escape. I will join you soon."

Jin just threw Leo into the arms of the guy in the middle. As he got on the back of guy in the middle, he spoke:

"Wait, what about my sis? She is still here."

Jin: "Don't worry, Leo. Your sister is safe back in Ranxus. You are going to meet her. This city is lost. I will be joining you in a few minutes. First, I need to take care of everyone here. (Looking at the other three, he spoke:) I will create a path for you. When I say, just dash forward and don't look back. Ready?"

As the other three nodded, Leo looked back at his friend Jay who was frozen to the ground watching all the commotion. Before Jay or Leo could utter a word, Jin struck the ground. The nexus symbol appeared underneath every person's foot and teleported them to a safe place. The next moment, Jin quickly spun around, circling his hands as he spun and another symbol appeared.

The symbol that had appeared was the same on his back and this time bigger in size, which covered the whole ground where the Xerkers stood. The circular pair of rings appeared again with larger blades, this time from beneath their feet and in an instant, the whole group of Xerkers just disintegrated into nothing.

This gave the other three a clear path to escape, and they took this moment and dashed forward. Those three quickly jumped into the air and from beneath their shoes; an air board quickly came out; half-half from each shoe and linked to each other around the core. In the middle of the air board was a hexagonal symbol connected to a small core that glowed red. The three of them took Leo and sped up on the air board into the sky.

Jin waited till everyone in the city was teleported to a safe place, and then he sped up towards the rest of his group. Just as Jin reached close to them, they were again surrounded. This time the guy who was carrying Leo closed his eyes and spun a full 180 degrees along with his air board, and a powerful tornado just twisted around, scattering the enemies. This allowed them to break through and dash forward. They sped further and further into the clouds, and suddenly, a bright flashlight blinded them and illuminated the whole sky.

Leo just stared at his surroundings. The light which had illuminated the sky was from the sun. Below them were the clouds, which looked like a soft fluffy bed to sleep on. They all sped forward, and as they sped, a structure could be seen at some distance which kept on getting bigger and bigger as they came closer. Leo was even more amazed at the structure and forgot about the pursuers at that moment. The big structure was none another than a big palace situated on the top of the hexagonal-shaped cloud.

On both sides of the palace were two large towns situated on two arrow-shaped blades, the same as the symbol on Jin's back. The arrow-shape extended from the hexagonal shaped cloud on which the palace was situated. There was a third town behind the palace.

Eight blades were covering the palace in the shape of ribs. On the top of the blades were hexagonal-shaped rings with arc headed blades at the edges of the rings. It was an utter beauty that couldn't be described or compared. Leo's mouth felt open as they reached in front of the palace. They all came down near the stone path in the open area and landed down. The air board seeped back into their shoes as they landed.

Leo suddenly lost his footing and fell on top of the girl who in turn fell to the ground with him. The next moment she punched him in the nose without realizing, as Leo had accidently grabbed her breasts as they fell. She spoke:

"What the hell Leo. Not a good time."

Leo stared at her while covering his nose which was bleeding now. The girl soon realized that it was an accident and she got up embarrassed at what she had blurted out suddenly. She gave him a kerchief to wipe his nose. They both apologized to each other. Watching this sudden comical, others burst into laughter. Leo covered his face as well, while the girl glared at Jin who was laughing the hardest.

Jin: "Hahaha! Be careful, Leo. You don't want to be squashed."

Jin felt the chills as the girl glared at him. He quickly avoided her gaze as he stood up and went near Leo and healed him.

Jin: "Before we go further (He turned towards Leo and spoke), I know we are kind of late on the introduction part but let me introduce my friends to you. The girl you see before you is Rose. On the right, the man is named Dan and on the left is Von. We all are Cloudscars. The kingdom you see before you is Ranxus. (Leo opened his mouth to say something, but before he could say, Jin continued) we know. The rest will be explained later. Come on! Let's go."

As they walked forward, Leo noticed the nexus symbol on both sides of the stone path ahead, and on top of it were statues of winged creatures that looked like human shapes hung in the air without any support. These creatures were big, and their wings were in the form of arc-triangle and the middle, a sword suspended without any support. One side of the wings was white coloured, and other side was black. Their upper body was covered with feathers of white and blue shaded petals. Leo was kind of scared at the sight of them and kept walking quite close to Jin. He turned towards Jin and asked:

"What are those? Those symbols were the same as the ones at my home and on your back as well."

Jin: "Those are called Nexus. Well, about them being there, you'll find out soon. And as for your home, I think only one person can explain that better than me. We are currently going to meet him."

They all stepped forward, and as soon as they took a step, the numerous winged creatures moved, and the sword came out of the wings and plunged into a hole at the tip of the nexus symbol. At once, petals of white and blue shade formed rib-like structures and covered their path. They walked down the path. Petals circled around them, forming an arc as they walked.

Jin: "Those are created from the core of the Earth. They are Cos, the protectors of this kingdom."

The next moment stars of light fell down on the group and the petals circling them. As soon as the light touched the petals, they were illuminated and gave a shiny light of shade of white and blue. Leo was mesmerized by what he saw, which helped him calm down his fear. Meanwhile, he didn't notice when they reached the gate.

The palace gate was of the same shape and symbol as on Jin's back. Although it was not so huge, the shape of the gate made it look huge. The gate suddenly broke into many triangular arced blades as soon as the group reached near them and flew at high speed towards the nexus symbol near them. There were no statues of cos on those nexus symbols, and those triangular arced blades struck those symbols with a huge impact that blew away the petals circling the group.

In the middle of the triangular arced blades, a small door opened, revealing an arc which quickly struck a black wall which stood where the palace gate was in the arc holes. All the arcs struck the black thing in the arc holes at the same time. There was a sound, and the black thing broke into many nexus shaped blades and just hung in mid-air. Just then, three figures walked in to view.

Chapter – 3

TWIN CORES

Part - I

In the middle was a woman, who had long violet and red shaded hair which reached till her upper back. Her ears were flat as if glued to her head. She had a round-shaped nose with three narrow slits, arc- shaped, extending from the edges and joined in the center like a triangle without sides above her wet lips. Her eyes were crystal blue with a shade of silver. Each of her shoulders had one pointy horn. Parts of her body were covered with white fur. Behind her lower back were two arced blades supported with a nexus hilt which were hung in an arced scabbard. She was holding a bouquet in her hands.

Behind her were two men who were of the same features as of the woman. They were walking at some distance behind the woman. The three reached near the group. Leo was finding it difficult to stare at the woman as she was emitting a bright radiance. He would steal a gaze at the woman once or twice and then look here and there. Jin, who saw Leo's nervousness, quickly smirked and nudged him in the shoulder and spoke:

"Don't be nervous, Leo; she is the commander of the army of Ranxus. Her name is Viola. She is the most capable, trustworthy and respectable person in the kingdom. Although she can be scary sometimes. (Jin came closer and whispered in his ear) She is a Riodine. A Riodine is one who is a half unicorn and half-human."

After speaking, he backed away quickly as Viola stepped closer. Leo looked at Jin, confused about his reactions and couldn't say anything. As he turned, Viola had reached near Leo and stood near presenting him the bouquet. Leo took it, and the woman bent down and kissed his forehead and spoke:

"Welcome back, Lord Leo. We have been waiting for your return. My men will guide you inside, and as for you (turning towards Jin, who shrugged a little), you are coming with me."

Before anyone could say anything, Viola had grabbed Jin and pulled him away from the group. Jin struggled to get free. Viola turned to Leo and spoke:

"Excuse us, Lord Leo, we have some matters to attend to."

Next moment Viola was seen dragging Jin into the palace. Everyone stared at the disappearing figure of Viola and Jin and smiled. Rose, who had been laughing, suddenly stepped forward and spoke:

"Hahahaha! Well, that's a sight I cannot miss."

Leo pointed towards the disappearing figure of Jin and asked:

"Is he going to be alright?"

Rose: "Ah, don't worry about him. He always gets in trouble anyway. Come on! Let's go. Master Taston is waiting to meet you."

Leo: "Master Taston? Who's that?"

Rose: "Just come, and you will see."

Rose stepped forward towards the entrance of the palace leading the group, were joined by the two men who had been following Viola. As they entered the palace, another mesmerizing surrounding made Leo freeze in his steps, and his mouth felt open.

The floor was made of clouds with four diamond-shaped pits with a silver crystal liquid on four sides, and extending from them were tunnels with a semi-circle shaped into the diamond-shaped gate-like structure in the form of a nexus symbol in the center. At the three sides in the middle corner were nexus symbols. Beyond those symbols were gates shaped in the same manner from which they had entered into the palace. The palace had no roof but a cyclone shaped cloud revolving at a high speed, and the light was entering the palace through narrow slits. In the end, from where the group stood, a person was standing.

He had the same features as that of the woman. He had nothing like blades. Instead, his arms were fully covered with silver runes and silver strings were coming out of the runes and connecting each other. He was kneeling down on one leg with his back turned towards the group. He was doing something with his hands as his index finger, and the middle finger were inserted into the cloud beneath, and his eyes were closed as if visualizing something. As the group reached near him, he opened his eyes and got up and, turning around, bowed with a smile. He had a gentle look on his face. As the others bowed back, Leo did the same.

Taston: "Welcome back Leo. My name is Taston. I am the keeper of the orange core also called Ranxus. You must be having many questions in your mind (as he read through the questioning face of him). Before I answer your questions, if you'll please follow me."

Leo: "Ummm.... Where is my sister?"

Taston: "Don't worry, Leo. Just follow me. She is safe and sound."

Taston walked forward towards the diamond gate in the center and stopped near it. He raised his hands and crisscrossed them in front of him, and the silver crystal liquid entered the tunnels and into the center of the diamond gate and as soon as the four sides met at the center, four pillars of the liquid formed at the four corners of the gate and it broke into four arced blades and flew down into the pit. There was a flash of light as they flew. A cyclonic cloud formed downward, and Taston beckoned everyone to follow him. Leo hesitated but seeing others follow, he also followed. As soon as Leo stepped into the cyclonic cloud, their feet touched on something soft.

As the cloud disappeared, Leo realized he was standing on top of a circular ring made of white marble. Around the ring were arc-shaped clouds floating in the air. On the top of the ring were six nexus symbols which were connected to six orange, flamed balls that were suspended in the air beyond the arc-shaped clouds. Just a few feet away from him was his sister Kate, who was waiting for him. As soon as she saw Leo, she ran and hugged him tightly.

Kate: "Leo, I am glad you are safe. (Turning around to others, she bowed and spoke:) Thank you! For bringing Leo back to me safe and sound. I am grateful."

Taston: "Don't worry about it, Lady Kate. It's our duty to protect you and Leo."

Taston continued:

"Now what I am about to tell you may be hard for you to understand right now, but you need to know everything. You, Lord Leo, are the Wingblade, the symbol of Ranxus."

Leo: "Wingblade? Symbol of Ranxus? What do you mean by that?"

Taston: "Wingblade means a person who is a Quabreed. Leo, you have the blood of four breeds. (Looking at his confused face, Taston further continued). Here let someone else explain from the beginning."

Taston (pointing with his hand to the center of the ring, spoke):

"Lord Leo, kindly step forward in the center of the ring. (Turning to Kate, he spoke:) Lady Kate, if you would follow me."

Kate stepped away from Leo, and Taston waved his hands and petals of white and blue enveloped both Taston and Kate. As the petals were enveloping both of them, Kate looked at Leo first then at Taston and spoke:

"Can't I stay with him?"

Taston: "Apologies Lady Kate. Only Lord Leo is allowed into the core and no one else. Don't worry. He won't be in harm's way. I can assure you that."

Kate looked at Leo again as she and Taston disappeared and reappeared back on the palace floor. Meanwhile, Leo was standing in the center. A bright light began to glow around the feet of Leo and a nexus symbol bigger than those at the six nexus symbols that were already on the ring. The bright light suddenly broke into six lines extending towards the six other nexus symbols, which in turn formed a chain that connected the six orange flamed balls and the balls glowed bright orange with high intensity.

Suddenly each ball broke into three 3-D blades and struck each nexus symbol in the three holes that appeared in the shape of the corners of a triangle. As soon as the blades struck, the center cracked open, and Leo fell right down into a bigger ball of orange flame, which was the core. Leo was able to breathe inside the core, and on top of that, he felt the warmth of the core, and he could hear the heartbeat of the planet.

Out of nowhere, numerous flares formed into the rope-like structure and entered Leo's body. He was covered in those flares and he just converged with the core and with a flash bright light, he disappeared. Next moment he was standing in the middle of the sea, where there was a raised triangular platform that seemed to be floating on the seawater surface. The size of the triangular platform was equal to the size of the 100 largest ships in the world put together in the form of a triangle. On top of the platform were crystallized glasses formed into a 3D triangle placed with their pointy sides facing upward and bases facing inside. Inside the triangle, there were four levels.

There were pipelines connected from all of the four levels in the triangle. The pipelines were further connected to three enormous crates that were also floating on the water surface at the three sides of the triangle. The crates supplied the resources to huge hexagonal rings that circled around the triangular structure beyond those crates. There were small containers attached with a house carved inside the hexagonal rings.

Leo practically walked on top of the water surface easily towards the platform through the circular pillars that connected the rings to each other. As he neared the platform, he touched the crystals and quickly, he was pulled inside.

He was standing inside the lowest level, which was completely filled with water. It was the available pure water that had been brought into the container and was cloned and distributed through a pipeline that was connected to a device kept in the middle. At the top of the roof of the bottom level, a pipeline was connected in the center into which water was flowing, and other pipes were also connected from the level to the crates outside.

Leo was taken to the third level, and it was the area for purifying the polluted air and supplying pure air into the cities. On the second level, varieties of crops. All types of fruits and trees were grown. In the 1st level, there were bright lights which seemed like a source of power that enabled the whole structure to function.

As Leo stared in awe at the structure, he didn't notice a stranger approach him from the back. He only noticed her when she reached beside him. Leo quickly stepped back, watching the figure whose face was fully water formed with blue sparkle eyes. Her body was fully transformed by the colour of moss and water. The figure sensed Leo's discomfort and spoke:

"Don't be scared Leo, I am the spirit of the "EARTH" or rather in a human language known as "TERRA". You must be having a lot of questions. I will answer them all."

Leo: "Spirit? I thought spirits never existed."

Spirit: "So you believe. But its true spirits do exist. Not everyone can see them. Only the ones who are connected to them can see them like you and me."

Leo: "What do you mean by I am connected to you."

Spirit: "Let me explain everything."

Chapter – 4

TWIN CORES

Part - II

"It all began with the formation of the universe. The big bang gave rise to the formation of the universe. Thus, when the universe was formed, it also had a core just like a planet has, which is called Cluster Nexus. In the cluster nexus, were born the very first living beings of the universe, the Cloudscars. They were the guardians of the Cluster Nexus. Slowly the universe expanded. Various galaxies, solar systems, stars, planets and other heavenly bodies formed. Even the almighty one known as the god came into being along with Cluster Nexus. In some parts of the universe, they believe that god's power comes from the core of the universe."

"Inside the core of the universe, there was a silver spirit by the name of Eraser, whose energy was very pure in silver colour. That energy was evil, and it was sealed with the utmost care by the pure spirit, Eternal of the Cluster Nexus. For many years, it remained dormant."

"Eraser's energy started going out of control due to a certain incident. It all started in a certain galaxy named Raven. The planets of that galaxy evolved in a way one could never imagine. But as they evolved, they slowly started consuming the natural resources of those planets at a faster rate. Slowly wars broke out between the countries, and when their planet's resources got exhausted due to the war, they turned towards other planets, and war broke out on those planets too over natural resources. As days continued, the atmosphere around those planets deteriorated, and the galaxy's energy became unstable. Soon the day came when the whole galaxy exploded into tiny pieces. The sudden destruction of the galaxy caused a sway in the stability of the core of the universe. No matter what Cloudscars tried, they couldn't stop the stability from deteriorating. This was just the beginning.

"Couple of other galaxies met the same fate. Eraser's energy started leaking. Many of the Cloudscars fell under her spell and turned evil, whom you know as Xerkers. And one day, a war broke out in the cluster nexus between Eraser and Eternal. The fight made the core so unstable that Eternal's energy just exploded along with the core, and she split apart into ten pieces of star runes. The pieces scattered all over the extreme corners of the galaxies."

"Those Cloudscars who escaped sought refuge on various planets and went into hiding waiting for the time of the uprising. After that, what happened, I don't know, as our consciousness is no more linked. I came to know later that one piece had somehow fallen to Earth, and it was being sought by a Xerkers who had come to know of its existence."

"This world's destruction began with humanity's foolishness. The structure you see before you, is humanity's last hope. There are only five structures like this one around the world. Long ago when humans were careless enough to let their mistakes shake up nature to such an extent that global warming took control of the whole planet and devastated it to such a length that most of the natural resources disappeared, leaving only a few areas with available resources. As human nature goes, a civil war broke out, fighting for resources. U.N. (United Nations) tried its best and helped the situation to calm down by bringing in a peaceful solution."

"U.N. had sent its panel of experts to all the areas of available natural resources. They surveyed each location and, in the end, decided to use the combination of hologram and cloning technology to duplicate and distribute the resources and ensure the survival of humanity. It took some time to convince all the countries of this project. In the end, it was approved, and the war came to an end."

"Thus, this structure came into existence. They reformed all types of technologies and brought them together, and created this structure to duplicate resources and distribute them across all the remaining cities. Took a lot of hard work and sweat. But this wasn't the end. No one knew that a storm was coming. After a long peaceful time, a stranger appeared."

The spirit pointed towards a stranger standing near the base of the triangle staring at it. The stranger was wearing a hooded cloak with its back towards Leo and stood there staring. No one else was able to notice the stranger. That's when the stranger stretched out the hand and was about to touch the base of the triangle when the spirit of terra jumped at lightning speed towards the creature.

The creature managed to duck in time and touch the base of the triangle. A flash of bright light and at once, the whole structure disintegrated into small bits of scraps, including the humans. Leo was shocked to see this. At the same time, the spirit had managed to nick off the hood from the stranger's face. At once, silver-coloured hair unfolded towards the creature's upper back. The face was covered with a half-mask that reached till the nose. The creature had eyes that were in the form of small narrow slits, vertically shaped with a purple pupil filling the whole slit and four small slits across both cheeks in a horizontal line. The creature was a girl. The rest of the body was covered with clothing made of space. She coughed as she stood to face the spirit.

The spirit stood in front of her and spoke:

"Who are you? What do you want here? Leave at once, or I will kill you before you can even touch anything else."

The girl: "I am the guardian of the Cluster Nexus. I have come here to reclaim the part of Eternal. I won't leave until I get the piece. Anyone who stands in my way will be eradicated."

The stranger had somehow learned that a star rune piece was on this planet.

Spirit: "Leave this planet at once or face the consequences."

The girl: “You must be Terra. I am not leaving until I have found the piece of Eternal. I will repeat once again. Give me the piece and I will leave your planet unharmed.”

Spirit: “I will never give it to you. If you try to harm the beings on this planet, I won’t let you leave alive.”

The girl quickly ran on the top of water towards the next city and was about to touch the city as she reached near it when the spirit flew towards her with tremendous speed and punched her so hard in the stomach and sent her into the sea and a huge splash formed where she fell.

As the girl emerged out of the sea, she spoke:

“Ahhh! Now you have gone and done it. Be prepared to die.”

Spirit: “Why are you doing all of this? If you are the guardian of cluster nexus, aren’t you supposed to protect all beings in the world?”

The girl: “Protect? That’s a heavy word. I have seen many beings do harm to their planets. Even humans are no different. I don’t know why Eternal did nothing.”

Spirit: “So what if those beings harmed their planets. Not all beings harm, some even protect. Not all are evil. As far as I know, Eternal’s spirit will never harm anyone because she loves all the beings and protects them.”

The girl: “I am not here to debate on some useless topic. Give me the piece quietly, and I will let everyone live.”

Spirit: “Never. I will never let you take the piece and destroy everything.”

The girl: "You think I need your permission? You are wrong. If you don't give it to me willingly, I will destroy this planet itself and take it."

Spirit: "Why do you want to reclaim it?"

The girl: "You know why. Since you were linked to cluster nexus, then you must know what happened there. I have come to reclaim the part of Eternal which was blown away in the explosion. I know it's hidden somewhere on Earth, and I won't allow anyone else to have it."

She just sprang at the structure again to destroy it. But before she could touch it, she was thrown off again by the spirit. Thus, a battle started to save the piece from being taken and the planet from being destroyed.

The spirit grabbed the girl by her hand and punched her face so hard that she crashed against a nearby rock and crushed it to pieces. The next moment the rock rubbles flew as the girl got up and caught the spirit by the neck and threw her across the sea into the land, crashing into the empty buildings. As the spirit flew, she caught the girl's leg with a rope made of wood which came out of her hand and pulled the girl along with her. They both crashed into the buildings with a tremendous force demolishing the buildings.

The spirit sprang up and pinned down the girl on the ground as she lay there injured. The spirit was about to smash her head again when suddenly the girl struck her hand on the ground and with a huge force, the spirit was thrown off her feet and landed far away. Rubbles flew in every direction, and dust clouds formed everywhere. As the dust cleared, the spirit was lying on the ground, too injured to move.

Despite her injuries, the girl stood up with much difficulty and enclosed her hands in a circular form, —a spell circle formed above the spirit. The spell circle had skulls dipped in blood with lots of stars revolving inside the spell circle forming two hexagonal entwined in a helical structure. A bright light emanated from the skulls and punched the ground where the spirit lay, binding her to the ground. The girl turned towards the sea to go near the triangular structure again. Suddenly out of nowhere, two unknown figures appeared who had similar features as her. They seemed to be the guardians too.

The girl: "Damn it. Jake and Ralph, you both found me, hah! Stop interfering with what I am doing. I won't allow you to get in my way."

Jake: "Reona, please stop this. Don't listen to Eraser."

Reona: "(laughs hard). This is just the beginning. Eraser has shown me the true meaning of being a guardian. These beings are not worthy of our protection. You already saw many beings destroy themselves. Join me, and let's avenge our home and protect it. I can't have them destroy cluster nexus due to their foolishness."

Ralph: "Guess you leave us no choice then. We will have to use the force then."

Ralph waved his right hand, and the spell circle disappeared. The spirit got freed, and she stood up facing Reona. Reona looked at both of them, irritated at the intrusion in her way. She just smirked and snapped her fingers. At once, a surge of electric charge was released into the Earth's surface. It activated all the nuclear missiles, which sped up towards their targeted destinations all over the world. Jake, Ralph and the spirit tried to jump forward to stop the missiles, but their paths were blocked by thousands of Xerkers.

The next moment there were huge explosions in many parts of the world. The nuke missiles had exploded. Reona and the Xerkers disappeared. Meanwhile, alarms sounded at the remaining four cities, and a barrier was erected around them. The missiles exploded onto the cities, but they escaped unhurt. However, the radioactive dust was released into the Earth's atmosphere in a tremendous amount.

Chapter - 5

TWIN CORES

Part - III

The next moment Leo and the spirit appeared back on the top of the circular ring.

Spirit: "That was the start of the apocalypse."

"Well, it all began with the nuke war that you just saw. After the explosion, the four cities still survived, though everything else just turned to rubbles and dust and even the water became poisonous. The radioactive dust that had been created due to the explosion of nuke missiles and the nuclear reactors which had burst had seeped into every nook and corner of the planet. It even seeped deep inside the soil into the planet's core. Half of the human population on land perished."

"Remaining half of the population had their features mutated. Some developed magical powers, some developed internal organ failures, while some remained immune to the effect. Many took refuge in underground cities, and the rest formed their territorial towns in the rubble cities."

"The radioactive dust just made the core unstable. As you know, every living thing has two sides: one dark and the other light. So, the core has the same. As it became unstable, it split apart into two. Just as this phenomenon happened, various portals opened, and different creatures like Cloudscars, Riodines and a couple of other races intruded on to the planet. These creatures were unaffected by the radioactive dust."

"As the core split, the energy that flowed into the cluster nexus also affected the core of the universe, making it unstable. That's when your grandfather Ralph and his brother Jake who were Cloudscars, used both of their powers to form two kingdoms known as Ranxus and Ruzone, also called the twin cores. The two kingdoms then formed a barrier around the core, keeping the cores apart from each other to protect the planet's destruction. If the cores are allowed to touch other, there will be a huge explosion that can destroy this planet and all along with it."

"All the creatures that intruded on to the planet settled down in the two kingdoms casting away the differences of their races. However, the humans had a tough call-in making decisions whether to accept the outsiders or not. Thus, a civil war broke out among all the different races. For days the bloodbath continued, and lands got drenched with blood. In the end, the leaders of each race came together and formed a truce and settled down together. Since Ranxus and Ruzone had not had much space for everyone to stay, two major cities were formed. One city under Ranxus and the other under Ruzone."

"Thus, reigned peace for a long time, and Earth was saved. However, there was no sign of Reona again. The rumour was that Reona had disappeared along with most of the Xerkers. As time moved on, Ralph got married to Shea, your grandmother, a Stardraco. Thus, your father Fes was born, half Stardraco and half Cloudscar, who later got married to your mother Lea, half Riodine and half Cyron. Then you were born Leo, a Wingblade, a Quabreed. You are one-fourth Stardraco, one-fourth Cloudscar, one-fourth Riodine and one-fourth Cyron."

Leo: "What's a Stardraco, Riodine and Cyron?"

Spirit: "Stardraco is a race of space dragons, Riodine is half unicorn and half-human while Cyron's have a story behind them. You will get to know about them as you go forward. Right now, it's not the time to let you know, and also, I am not the right person for it. And as for Cloudscar, you already know."

"When you were born, it was prophesized that you would bring peace to the universe and destroy the dark side of the cluster nexus. Around the time when you were born, your father Fes brought Kate home. No one knew anything about her true identity, and she seemed to have lost her memory, which I found way too weird. But can't blame her for losing her memory as she was found by your father lying unconscious on the ground."

Spirit: "Well continuing, I forgot to tell you one thing, when Ralph formed the kingdom Ranxus, I merged my powers with Ralph. So, you have my power too inside you. That's how we are connected."

"After one year of your birth, Jake just disappeared all of a sudden. No one knew the reason why he disappeared leaving Ruzone to be managed by your father. Just around when you were ten years old, Kate went crazy as if she lost control of herself and some kind of silver energy emanated from her and exploded inside Ranxus. I don't know myself as to what happened to her. But something seemed sinister. There was no choice but to drop the barrier of the core to let the explosion into the air. That's when Jake appeared in Ranxus along with a few Xerkers and launched an attack on you and your parents. You and your parents, with few Riodines who were protecting you, were trapped inside the palace with Jake and Xerkers, and Kate had fainted as your father lay holding her."

Jake: "Hello, nephew! Let go of Leo. If you give him to us, we will let you and your wife go."

Fes: "Why, uncle Jake? What happened to you? Why are you doing this?"

Jake: "I was awakened to the reality. You better do as I say if you all want to live."

Fes: "No, uncle. You are being deceived. Please turn back at once. We can't let you have Leo."

"Fes stepped forward, covering Leo and Lea behind him. Jake waved his hand, and all the Riodines protecting Leo exploded from within, and flesh pieces and blood lay everywhere. The next moment Jake disappeared and reappeared in front of Fes and Lea and just pierced his hand into Fes's chest and crushed his heart. While he held Lea by her neck in his right hand, trying to strangle her. I tried to get out and help, but I couldn't as a spell was cast to hold me in. Even I tried to transfer my energy to you, but the spell was strong, and it had a feeling of the same silver energy that emanated from the cluster nexus."

"That's when the Xerkers surrounded you and enclosed their hands into a pentagon shape, and your body was pierced with Xeton rods. There was a huge explosion, and everyone was thrown off. Lea suddenly disappeared with you and Kate as Taston made way to the inner palace when the spell cast to keep everyone out lifted with the explosion."

"We had a feeling you were still alive somewhere, but no matter what, we couldn't find you all until today. May I know what happened to Lea?"

Leo: "I don't know. All I remember is sis Kate raised me from my childhood. I asked sis too, but she too didn't know anything about mom."

Spirit: "Well, no worries. I hope you unveil the remaining questions on the way. I think I have told you everything. It's time for you to leave and join others."

Leo: "Wait, what about when I was pierced with those Xeton rods? How did I survive that?"

Spirit: "Alas, even I don't know the answer to that. Time will answer your remaining questions. Don't worry. I will always be watching over you. As for the piece of Eternal, it went missing with the explosion. I don't know anymore where it is hidden. Find it, Leo, before Xerkers have it."

"One more thing Leo. I will be watching Kate and make sure nothing like that happens again."

Leo: "I don't believe sis would do anything like that."

Spirit: "I want to believe that too but unfortunately, circumstances point to her. I am sorry Leo."

Leo was sad on hearing it but he knew she could be right. He bowed and just disappeared into a mist of white and blue petals and reappearing back on the palace floor where Taston and Kate were waiting for him.

Taston: "Well, Lord Leo, I hope she answered all of your questions. If not, fear not. You will find them on your way. Both of you get some rest for now. Tomorrow is going to be the start of a bright new day. If you follow me, I will take you to your house."

Kate and Leo followed Taston out of the palace doors. This time they stepped out of the palace door in the opposite direction to the one they had entered in at first. The door just broke into many triangular arced blades and flew at high speed towards the nexus symbol beyond the door.

They stepped out of the door and the door sealed back with all the triangular arced blades flying right back and forming the door. There was an open path that led to a huge spiral-shaped town, surrounded by helically shaped forest. Eight blades that were covering the palace in the shape of ribs looked way too magnificent and gigantic as Leo walked beneath it. Hustling of busy streets could be heard in the distance. As they neared the gates of the town, the five rings flew into the air and struck the ground near them in a semicircular manner.

A hexagonal-shaped ring formed around the group and engulfed them in white light. As the white light diminished, the group entered the town gates. Leo and Kate's mouths fell open with what lay beyond those gates.

Chapter – 6

FALLEN CORE

The gate was made of crystallized water, and the walls around the town were made of clouds. As they stepped inside the gate, Leo and Kate felt something slippery against their feet. As they both looked down, they noticed floors made of water. The water was flowing in circles. However, their feet didn't get wet. In the middle of the circle was a fountain, a strange one at that. There was a huge ring on the floor. In the ring, the floor had tiles of petals with a diamond-shaped hole in the center. The tiles were placed vertically at a certain distance apart, forming a hexagonal shape together.

Water sprang out of them and flowed outward in the form of a gun in a helical shape towards the top and at the top formed a circle. From the circle, it sprang outward towards the nearby ground. The water sprang on Leo, Kate and Taston too, but they didn't get wet. Instead, the water drops just passed through them onto the floor. As they passed the fountain awestruck with wonder, they further saw something so amazing that made them freeze in their steps.

There were two water floored paths connected to circular rings beyond those paths. The circular rings were spherical in shape and were made of water too. Water was flowing rapidly through rings and houses made of wood with bases covered with clouds situated at the edges of the rings. The circular ring was wide enough for many to go through at once. There were further more circular rings towards the top. The whole structure formed into a conical shape. In the middle of the rings were six wooden trees that formed a helical structure from the top and met at the bottom where a water portal formed. Paths from each house met at a hole in the trees.

As Leo, Kate and Taston reached one of the paths, three surfboards formed made out of clouds. Taston got on one and beckoned Leo and Kate to get on the other two. As soon as three of them got on the boards, they sped up with high speed. As they sped, they passed through the holes in the trees. Leo noticed inside the hole on both sides were portals made of water. They kept on speeding towards the top. As they sped, they noticed wooden houses at the edge of the path situated on top of the cloud. Many passers-by greeted them as they went.

As they sped further, they saw at the edge of the town were five finger-shaped structures in the form of hexagonal-shaped rings. Finally, Taston stopped at a house that was almost near the top, and so did Leo and Kate. All three of them got off their boards and stepped onto the empty area of the wooden floor of the house which lay in front of the door. The door in front was made of water crystals. As soon as

Leo neared the door, the crystals broke into triangular spears piercing the bodies of Kate and Leo without flinching any wound as if absorbed into their bodies.

Taston: "Water crystals. They become part of you and live inside as you continue to stay in your house. Once you leave your house, they come out from your body and transform back into the door again. Don't worry as the crystals enter your body, a water barrier is raised in the place of the door and around the house to prevent anyone else from getting in unless it's a friend it recognizes. The water barrier has the property of x-raying the whole body of a being including the inner thoughts, character and physical part too for any kind of ill intentions."

Leo: "Cool."

Taston smiled and indicated with his hand to them to go inside. Leo noticed a circular ring with a transparent liquid of white and red-orangish light in the ceiling as he stepped inside. Beyond the ring, the ceiling was made of pure glass pieces that fell onto the floor and disappeared automatically as soon as they touched the ground. A bright white light appeared from the circular ring, and the whole ceiling lit up. The glass pieces fell, emitting that white light. It was an amazing sight. Leo and Kate looked bewildered.

Taston: "Ranxus absorbs the moonlight and sunlight and emits it as the power for the houses and the palace."

All the furniture lay the same as it was at Leo's house, with the support of the same nexus symbol. Leo turned towards Taston and pointed out:

"I have always wondered about these symbols that I have seen from my childhood, and even in my dreams, I have seen them. What are those?"

Taston: "Those are nexus symbols that represent the core. They harness the energy of the core and distribute it to the whole world. The spirit and your grandfather formed this symbol to prevent the surge of energy released from the unstable core from destroying everything."

Leo: "That means only natural power is the source of every electronic device that works. Is that right, Master Taston?"

Taston: "Just call me MT. Yes, you are right Lord Leo. Now rest up. Tomorrow morning will be a new start for you both. See you both tomorrow. Good night."

Leo and Kate: "Good night MT."

Taston walked out of the front door and disappeared while Leo and Kate settled down in their new house, as Leo filled in Kate all that he and Terra had talked about except the part where Kate had silver energy emanated from her. They both had dinner and settled down. They found the same spectacles that they had in their home lying on a wooden table nearby. They wore it and started watching an old movie falling asleep while watching.

Leo just suddenly woke up. It was dark for him to see anything. A bright light appeared in front of him. He called for Kate, but there was no reply. He realized; it came from a door. He walked towards the door and entered it. As he stepped outside the door, his feet touched the blood-stained ground, with flesh pieces lying around everywhere. In front of him was a core that he later realized was the heart of the universe blazing with the fury of the silver energy. A spirit emerged from that heart.

The spirit was draped with the clothing of different stars and galaxies. Her face was the same as Kate. She stood before Leo, gazing her intense fury at him. As she raised her right hand, Leo was grabbed with chains from the stars that had gathered around him. She enclosed her hand in a circular form, and a spell appeared above Leo's head with skulls on it, and his energy was being sucked out of his body into the circle.

Leo's body started deforming as all of his body's energy was being absorbed through the magic spell into the core, and the energy was so intensely evil that every planet overflowed with the evil energy. Instantly who came in contact with the energy either got disintegrated or fell to the energy. Leo just screamed up and woke up sweating.

Kate was sitting by his head, wiping his face and calling his name again and again. She held him as he woke up. Leo hugged her tightly, scared by what he saw. Kate caressed him and calmed him down.

Kate: "It's alright, Leo. Everything is alright. You are safe. Get up and Wash up."

Kate kissed Leo's forehead and went back into the kitchen. While Leo walked to the bathroom. The bathroom was spacious but similar to the bathroom at his house. He quickly freshened up and came out. Sitting by Kate's side, he looked at her. Kate noticed him staring at her. She looked at him and asked:

"What's wrong, Leo? You seem a bit tensed about something."

Leo: "(Smiled and spoke) Nothing, sis. Everything is fine. Just was wondering what is going to happen now."

Kate touched his face while smiling and spoke:

"Don't worry. No matter what happens, I will always be by your side and protect you."

Leo also smiled and relaxed on her lap, and slowly, he fell fast asleep. The next morning, they both woke up with Jin calling out to them. Jin, Rose, Von and Dan had come together to take Leo and Kate back to the palace for their coronation. Leo and Kate both woke up as they stared at Jin and his group's faces sleepily.

Jin: "Yo. We came to get you. Get ready."

Leo went in to freshen up while Kate invited Jin and his group to settle down for breakfast. As Leo stepped out of his bathroom onto the nexus symbol at the doorstep, a new set of clothes that were made for him appeared. He had a shade of sunlight and moonlight colour on a cape-like clothe which wrapped around on both of his legs in an entwined helical structure on each leg. There was a circle of very small holes barely visible to eyes, each situated at a certain distance apart. There were four kinds of that circle on each leg. On his legs appeared bandages that wrapped around both of his feet, completely covered.

On his upper body appeared a sleeveless shirt and with the symbol of an entwined half sun and half-moon in a mixed circular structure. Beneath the shirt, his body was covered with a cape with slits on both sides. The collars of the cape stood up to cover his neck and both sides of his throat. Through the shoulder part where there were no sleeves, a cape entwined with the same colour of sunlight and moonlight entwined together draped his arms till the wrist where they formed in the form of gloves with claws at the end of the gloves. His hair formed a sideway slanting style. He looked very handsome.

As for Kate, she was wearing the same pants and the same armour as Leo. On top of the armour, she wore a top with shoulder less clothing. In the center of the clothing was a circular spiral shape of the sun and moon rays entwined together. Both the sleeves spiralled on her arms till her fingers and the end of the sleeves wrapped around each of her fingers. The top was made of crystal water. She looked stunning.

Jin and his group were wearing the same clothes as they wore on the day they saved Leo and Kate. Rose looked so lovely, as Leo remembered when he first met her. Leo still stole glances at Rose in between. Rose noticed Leo's stare and smiled back at him blushingly. Others noticed this and smiled among themselves. While Jin slapped on Leo's back and joked:

"Come on, Leo, enough with the stare. You are going to melt a volcano. Hahaha"

All of them laughed while Rose and Leo turned red. Rose gave Jin a scornful look which gave him chills and reminded him of Voila. Soon they got back on the surfboards made of clouds and sped down towards the holes in the trees. As they neared the holes, Leo and Kate saw Jin and the others just jump into the portals and disappear. Leo and Kate did the same, and they felt squishiness as they jumped into the portals. The next moment, they were back on the marble ring in the palace. Taston and Terra were standing right next to him. Around them stood three races: Riodines, Humans and Cloudscars. The beings from those three races were chosen by Terra herself to reside on Ranxus and protect it based on their personality, their powers and their righteousness.

Everyone bowed their heads in welcome to their King Leo and Queen Kate. Taston beckoned Leo and Kate to step forward towards the center of the ring. As they walked forward towards the center, spiral shape petals of white and blue appeared around the ring. The petals flew right into the hands of Taston and started twisting in his hands. A crown made with a shade of night sky, and the moon formed in his hands, and he placed it on top of Kate's head. Everyone cheered for their queen.

The next moment the petals flew again into the hands of Taston, forming another crown made with a shade of the bright blue sky and the sun and just he was about to place it on top of Leo's head, the whole ring shook terribly. Everyone froze, and the crown fell down and broke into petals. The next moment Leo rushed to Kate, calling her loudly:

"Sis...... Sis......."

Kate was trembling from head to foot and screaming. The spirit understood. She raised her hands to pin down Kate, but before she could even move, there was a bright light from Kate, and the whole place exploded with a tremendous blast. Everyone was thrown off, and the whole of Ranxus exploded. Everyone got separated. Just then, Jake and the Xerkers appeared and attacked and killed many of them. Jin and others tried to regroup and save Leo, but it was too late.

Kate had appeared near Leo and thrust her fist many times into his body, badly injuring him and kicking him hard down into the ocean. Leo stared back at Kate as he faded into unconsciousness. Ranxus had fallen, and Leo's body just washed up the sea to no one knows where. Ranxus lay in rubbles with everything destroyed by the explosion. Kate and Jake stood on the marble ring with the spirit tied up to a pillar of Xeton, which was pentagonal in shape with orange flares wrapped in a spiral shape.

Kate: "Finally, I am free. Time to conquer the universe and bring Eternal glory to the cluster nexus."

Chapter – 7

REUNION

It suddenly started raining. It seemed as if the clouds were crying, feeling sad for the fallen Ranxus. In the heavy rain, a voice echoed somewhere far deep near the ocean in a faraway place:

"Twin clusters of nexus, shine your bright wind;

Reel in the ray of hope, bring back the life that was lost;

Let the drop of each blood make the path for the ultimate glory."

A woman walked towards a body floating in the water. The body was none other than Leo's. She held him in her arms and took him to a hole in a tree nearby, and entered into a portal in the tree. The next moment she arrived in an underground town. The town was normal as a regular human town with houses situated in a circular shape with a big spell circle with skulls on it in the center of the town. There were pathways between the buildings to move from one lane to another. Watching the woman, the townsfolk greeted her, and she greeted back but didn't wait to talk. She just took him to a hut just right where the spell circle lay.

The hut was average and was made out of trees entwined together to form a hut. She put Leo on the bed and raised her hands as a magic circle formed on top of him made out of blood. There were orange balls on the circle. They emitted out blood which flowed into Leo, and the blood regenerated Leo's wounds back and healed it. Leo twitched a little but couldn't open his eyes since he had lost too much blood and had received a blow mentally.

The woman kept on healing Leo all night. By morning Leo had completely healed but was still weak to get up. He opened his eyes barely and was seeing blurrily. He heard a woman's voice and thinking it was Kate and everything was a dream, he spoke:

"Sis.... Sis... Is that you?"

Woman: "Relax, Leo. You need to rest. Let's talk when you feel fine."

The woman just rubbed Leo's forehead gently. Feeling the warmth of her hand, he fell back asleep. In his sleep, he felt falling down his memory lane. He found himself staring at himself while he was a child before the attack on Ranxus occurred. He seemed around ten years old. He was lying under a tree staring at the night sky gleaming with stars. His hands at the back of his head and his legs crisscrossed. Suddenly a lock of golden hair covered his face, and a familiar face just crept near his face. It was so sudden that

Leo got startled and got up. Their heads smacked. Writhing with pain, Leo spoke:

"Ow ow ow. Rose, seriously, stop doing that every time."

Rose: "Come on, Leo. It's just for fun. Geez, scaredy-cat."

Leo: "I am not. I just got startled."

Rose: "Meh."

Leo: "Anyway, Rose, where were you? Weren't you supposed to be here a couple of hours earlier? I have been waiting for you."

Rose: "Sorry, Leo. I got held up in my training. What were you doing anyway, staring at the sky?"

Leo: "Oh nothing, just staring at the stars."

Rose: "Ohooo. You know when someone stares at stars a lot, it means he is thinking of someone."

Leo: "I.... I.... am not remembering anyone."

Rose: "Then why are you stammering."

Rose poked Leo and ran away as Leo got up and chased her. Leo caught her hand, but as she attempted to release her hand, she tripped and fell, taking Leo along with her. The soft grass swayed as they fell to the ground with a soft sound. Their faces were inches from each other. They both turned red and got up.

Rose: "Sorry that went too far. Let's just go home."

Leo: "Yeah (couldn't look at her as he was blushing). Let's go."

As they both started walking, stars from the sky started falling in flames towards the ground. A star in flames also fell right on top of them, but in time Leo pushed rose away and then as the flame star- struck Leo, he suddenly woke up, now wide awake enough to see around. His eyes scanned the ceiling. The ceiling was made of wooden crystals that emitted bright sunlight inside the room. He turned his head around and saw that the inside of the house was circular in shape with a bed in the center. Around the bed, a pentagram was drawn as if a barrier had been erected. Beyond that was normal household furniture with usual household items. The items and furniture were very unfamiliar to Leo and seemed like the remnants of the world before destruction. His eyes met the woman who had saved him, now wiping his sweaty face.

She had strange eyes. She had four crisscrossed eyes with no eyeball but instead a single eyeball in the center of the crisscross. She had no nose. Her lips were wet like raindrops. Her hair was slanted sideways, and her back hair was long, which reached half of her back. Her hair had a shade of orange and white same as Jin's eyes. On her upper body, she wore a cape with wide slits over her arms and sides. Frontside in the center, there was something on the cape. It looked like a rune in the form of flares coming out of two blades.

On both sides of her shoulders were long horizontal slits reaching to the side of the throat on both sides. On both of her hands were small runes made out of the blood. Her lower body was covered with pants made of moonlight and sunlight with small slits at random places where wing-shaped rings formed. She just bent over and smiled at Leo and spoke:

"There, you will be fine now."

Leo: "Lady, who are you? The last time I remember...... (Clutching his head which was hurting)."

Woman: "Calm down, Leo. Rest a bit. Let's talk later."

Leo closed his eyes and gently fell back asleep. The woman just rubbed his head again and walked out of the room, closing the door behind her. The next morning, Leo was able to sit up. He was feeling better. He now looked around and noticed the room was somewhat similar to the bedroom that he had seen in his history books at school before coming to Ranxus. Just then, the door opened, and the woman walked in carrying a tray that looked like breakfast.

The woman came up to Leo and sat there as she placed the tray on top of a table beside the bed. She touched Leo's cheeks and smiled and spoke:

"My name is Lea. I am your mother, Leo. No matter how hard I tried, I couldn't stop the path from opening for you. I am glad you are better now. Did Kate do all of this?"

Leo was suddenly taken aback when he heard the woman who saved him was his mother. He was speechless and stared at her. Suddenly he hugged her tightly as tears ran down his cheeks. Lea caressed his head and gently rubbed his shoulder. Finally, Leo calmed down.

Leo: "Yes, she did. Where have you been all this time, mother? Did you know about Kate too? Why didn't you prevent it from happening?"

Lea: "I am sorry, Leo. When Fes, your father, found Kate, she had lost her memories or rather suppressed them. I don't know the reason, but Fes and I couldn't accept killing her, so we brought her back and raised her as your sister. We tried to raise her in the right way so that she would forget about the evil way. But I guess we couldn't prevent it after all. Sorry, you had to suffer because of our mistakes."

Leo: "No, mom. It wasn't your fault. You did what you thought was right. Besides, I know sis is still alive inside somewhere. I just have to bring her out of the dream. I missed you so much."

Lea: "I am sorry, Leo. I have missed you very much too. When I escaped with you from Ranxus while Fes died protecting us. I sealed up your presence to hide you and prevent you from being killed again. The last time I saw you stabbed with Xeton rods, I was heartbroken and thought I had lost you until you rose up unharmed, which was way too miraculous. After sealing your presence, I had wiped Kate's memory as well. Also, I had to research what had happened to you after being stabbed with Xeton rods because it's not easy to live through after being stabbed with nexus's power."

"After I left you, I immersed myself deep in the research of the cluster nexus and found that when you were stabbed with those rods, all of your organs had been destroyed and torn into shreds. But those rods had the property of renewing life. So, the rods dissolved into your blood along with your torned organs. Thus, you came back to life. Now you have become immortal and will live forever until the nexus of the universe remains."

"You will only die under three conditions:

The first would be if the nexus of the universe is destroyed, which may be near to impossible. Second, if you are stabbed again with those rods dipped in dark matter. But it may injure you seriously or kill you no one knows. Third, if your blood is drained out of your body."

"Until any of these conditions are met, you won't die and will be immortal. I know it has been hard for you, but forgive me for leaving for so long. I have always watched you from the shadows. I hope you will forgive me."

Leo smiled and held her hand on his cheeks. Lea smiled back and just fed him breakfast with her hand. She wanted to make him feel loved. She was really happy to see him again. Two days later, he was able to walk again as his strength returned. The day came when Leo wanted to leave and find Jin and others, but Lea stopped him.

"Leo, not now. You need to train yourself. While you were resting and recovering, I was gathering information as to what was happening outside. Ranxus has indeed been destroyed. Now Kate rules the outer world. She is trying to combine both the cores. When that happens, everything will be destroyed. But to combine both will take some time since it needs a tremendous amount of energy and also requires the piece of Eternal."

"The whereabouts of a piece of Eternal are unknown, but while you are undergoing your training, I will try to search for the information. They believe that you are not dead, so they are searching for you. For now, hide here as long as you can. Everyone here will protect you. Train here and become stronger. Follow me, Leo. I will take you to your training place."

Lea walked outside the hut, followed by Leo. As both of them stood at a few steps distance from the hut, Lea just punched the ground with her fist, creating a spell circle, and suddenly the ground around the hut started shaking. The skulls spell circle just rotated at high speed. A huge beam of light formed.

Lea: "Come, Leo."

Lea just beckoned with her hand to Leo to walk inside. He just followed his mother into the beam of light, and the surroundings just vanished. The next moment, Leo's feet just touched something solid.

Chapter - 8

REVELATIONS

Part - I

Leo found himself standing on the top of a straight bridge slab that was connected to a blue portal at the other end, just like the one they had entered from. There was another bridge slab that crossed at the center and was connected to two other portals. There was a circular slab of black colour with small holes shaded blood red. The width of the circular slab was not much but enough for two people to stand on. Lea started walking forward towards the center, followed by Leo. There was nothing but empty black space surrounding the place.

Leo: "What kind of place this is, mom?"

Lea: "This is the training ground created by me. So that people living here could train themselves to become stronger. Leo, before we begin your training, you need to know certain things. I suppose Terra must have told you lots of things."

Leo: "Yes, mother, she did tell me, but she also said I would learn certain things with time."

Lea: "Ok, Leo. Now listen carefully:

"Even though the Cloudscars were the guardians, they couldn't protect every planet as the universe had become vast. So, to protect each planet that had life, a race known as Cyron were chosen. Each Cyron was granted a zodiac power to watch over the planets and protect them. Planet earth had also been granted 12 zodiacs to protect it. The number of zodiacs is random and depend on planets that have lived in a solar system."

"But all above the zodiacs, there are five legendary zodiacs, namely: Zodiac of Celestial Spirits, Zodiac of Life, Zodiac of Time, Zodiac of Death and Zodiac of Energy. These five zodiacs stood above all other zodiacs and kept the order among them. But Eternal knew that there can always be a turnover. So, she shared another type of power with your great grandfather, known as the anti-zodiac. The anti-zodiac gives you the power to destroy all the other zodiacs if they tried to harm any living creature or Eternal herself."

"Leo, you have inherited those powers too. Kate also has the legendary zodiac power as she is the granddaughter of the being who had the power of the zodiac of celestial spirits. She is possessed by Eraser, so she has tremendous power inside her, and she is the most powerful being in the universe now. Only you can defeat her. That's why this training is necessary to bring out your true potential. It's going to be tough training, so don't push yourself too hard, honey. Also, I am going to try to see if I can find out about the whereabouts of the piece of Eternal as well as your friends. I hope they are all fine.

Do you have any questions?"

Leo: "Yes, mother. I thought sis was a Cloudscar?"

Lea: "No Leo. She was adopted by Cloudscars and raised up. There was an attack on the planet of Cyrons. One day, the Zodiac of celestial spirits just destroyed the planet. In the end Cloudscars interfered and stopped Kate's grandfather but it was too late. No one knew why he suddenly went berserk. But he killed many Cyrons and the other legendry Zodiacs. As the Cloudscars stopped him, that's when they found Kate as well."

Leo: "Ah, I see. But mom, sis is really a good person. She would do anything to harm anyone."

Lea:" I know Leo. She has just come under the influence of Eraser. You have to save her."

Leo: "I will do my best to become strong and save sis before anything worse happens to her."

Lea: "Do your best. I will leave you for now. Good luck, Leo."

Lea kissed Leo's forehead and retreated to the portal they had entered from, and she disappeared. He watched his mother disappear. As soon as his mother disappeared, four figures just popped out of the portal. They were completely space coloured. They came near him. The one on the right-side spoke to him:

"Hello Leo, we are the same as you. The four of us represent each breed of you. Together we are you. We will train you to become stronger and surpass yourself. We can't take your real appearance as we are just a form of space energy that comes depending on the person who came here to train. Right now, it's you, so we are here. For now, we will train your mind, heart and body first."

"Any power needs a clear and calm mind. But in your case Leo, you need to keep a balance between anger and calm to be in control of your power. So, we will work on that first. I would like to ask you to sit down in the center and close your eyes. Clear mind of any thought."

Leo tried, but he couldn't clear his mind.

Leo: "I can't. It's difficult to clear the mind. When I close my eyes, I think of my sis and everyone else."

The spirit spoke:

"Don't worry. You are thinking of them because you are worried. But do you know that if you don't get stronger, you will not be able to protect them? So, keep trying until you succeed. Think of all the happy memories you had with those people and then try to clear your mind. It will work."

Leo closed his eyes and was trying to clear his thoughts when suddenly a bright light flashed in his mind, and he fell unconscious.

Meanwhile, on the marble ring in Ranxus,

Kate was standing looking at the sky, which was visible now. The marble ring had risen with the castle destroyed, and all towns turned to rubbles. Terra was right beside her, bound by chains, unable to escape. Kate was dressed in clothing of dark purple colour with a symbol of circular arc-shaped arrow blades in silver colour on the left top side of the half top she was wearing. In the front, a tattoo of arc-shaped slits was extending from the chest to the abdomen on the left and right side. In the middle was a circular maze shaped structure from which arc-shaped tattooed blades were connected, shining bright silver.

Her eyes were narrow and of bright purple colour, and instead of a nose, had long slit across on both of her cheeks which opened and closed like a fish's mouth. She had a symbol of hexagonal-shaped arc headed arrow blades tattooed on her face with silver energy emitting from her body and her hair had turned silver. She now looked like the same person that Terra had showed Leo. Suddenly another Xerker appeared behind her and knelt down and spoke:

"My queen, the cities have fallen, and all the beings that dwelt in the cities are now our prisoners. Shall we execute them?"

Kate: "Not now. There is still use of them. What of Ruzone?"

Xerker: "All set, my queen. The only thing left is to start the process."

Kate: "Good. Any news from Ilov?"

Xerker: "No news yet. Shall I send someone to him?"

Kate: "No need, I will go myself. After all, those beings can never be lightly taken. Wait for me here. I will be back soon."

Xerker: "Yes, my queen."

He disappeared. While Kate whistled, a huge winged creature appeared. Its body had red scales and, on its back, in the middle, there were hexagonally connected diamond-shaped space-coloured scales. The same shape of scales was on its stomach in the middle. Its tail's end was H-shaped. Its face was also reds scaled with four horns and eyes in the form of slits. It was a space dragon. She got on the top of the dragon, and as soon as she stood in the middle of the hexagonal ring. The space-coloured scales emitted ropes in the form of space-coloured flares and wrapped around her waist, and her feet sank knee-deep into the dragon's back, and it just flew away. It could camouflage according to the environment and turn invisible along with its rider. That way, the enemies wouldn't spot it.

The dragon just flew so fast that a path was carved out in the clouds like a knife had been pierced through, creating a clean path. After flying a couple of minutes, the dragon landed on the ground on the land which belonged to the country of America. Now it lay in ruins. There were rubbles everywhere and torn down houses though it was still habitable with broken roofs and everything looked worn down due to war and exhaustion of resources. Even green moss was visible on the walls and floors in some places.

Kate got off the dragon and walked straight into a house just in front of where she had landed. The door was hanging in half, so she just pushed it slightly, which made the door break down into pieces with a loud noise. The front wall just split open into a circular shape, and dozens of cloaked figures with their face hidden with a hood entered the room.

It was so quick that Kate couldn't move a finger. She was surrounded. One of them stepped forward and spoke in a coarse voice:

"We know who you are. And you are not welcome here. What business do you have here?"

Kate: "Where is the messenger that I sent here? First, I would like to speak with him."

Cloaked Figure: "You mean this guy?"

The cloaked figure brought the severed head of the Ilov, the messenger that was sent by Kate. Kate was furious, but she knew if she made a mistake now, it would mean an unnecessary war which she didn't want to go for now. She just glared at them and spoke:

"How dare you do this to one of my people?"

Cloaked Figure: "We are no part of your war. You already know we stay neutral then why did you try to push us into it? We only join a side if that side offers us good rewards. Also, we were bored and needed a sport. That's why we killed him."

Kate: "Join me, and you will be rewarded with whatever you wish. How about it?"

Kate was just playing along for now, but she had other thoughts regarding their fate after the war.

Cloaked Figure: "What we wish in return is to kill Eternal. That has been our wish for centuries."

Kate: "Oh, I all know about you and Eternal. Castaway from your planet and banished by Eternal for destroying a planet in thirst of power. Don't worry. I will give you a chance to kill her. I need you to kill a certain someone named Leo. He is the Wingblade. If he dies, can Eternal be killed. Though I don't know where he is now."

Cloaked Figure: "We are tempted. But remember this, if you double-cross us, we will not leave you alone. Don't worry. We will find him and kill him. (Turning to two figures behind him and spoke:) Release them. (Turning to Kate) Do you have anything of his that can help me track him down?"

Kate gave him a cloth that she had used to wipe his sweat when he had nightmares. The cloaked figure gave that to a man behind him who whistled, and two birds came flying to him. The bird had no eyes and only a nose. It had wings with pointy spikes coming from the end of the wings, and it had human legs. The bird smelled the cloth and flew away. The cloaked figure then spoke:

"Don't worry, those creatures will find them. You can go back now and leave the rest to us. Our deal is in motion."

Kate: "Alright then. Keep me posted about your progress."

Kate turned around and walked to her space dragon. She mounted on it and flew away back to her place. She never meant to fulfil the wishes of those cloaked figures. Meanwhile, the cloaked figure, along with two of his subordinates, went after the birds leaving the rest back at their hideout.

Meanwhile,

Leo woke up only to find himself back in Lea's hut. And Lea was sitting right beside him, caressing his hair. She smiled when their eyes met, and Leo smiled back. Leo tried getting up, but his head hurt badly, so he lay back down while Lea was holding his head gently.

Lea: "Rest well, Leo. It seems like you really passed out back then."

Leo: "I don't know, mother. When I was told by them to close my eyes, I just blanked out and met with Eternal's energy spirit."

Chapter – 9

REVELATIONS

Part - II

Lea: "What did she say to you?"

Leo: "When I blanked out, I found myself in a space wrap. There she was, a pure blinding light standing right in front of me. I couldn't see her properly due to the blinding light, but she had such a purity that I felt warm. She was the energy spirit from the piece of Eternal that was on Earth. She mentioned Kate, the silver energy and everything else. She also told me the piece was hidden in a loophole, and it was a location in Central India."

Lea: "Did you just say India?"

Lea shivered at the mention of the name. Leo was worried at the sight of his mother shivering at the mention of the name.

Leo: "What's wrong, mother?"

Lea: "I have heard bad rumours about India. Let me consult someone. I will let you know what I find out. Rest now and get back your strength. You are going to need it."

Leo fell asleep, and Lea walked out of her hut and closed the door behind her and directly walked towards another hut which was situated at a distance. It was a normal human-made hut, and she knocked on the door. A very old man opened the door and asked her to come in. She went inside but didn't sit and turned around and looked at him and spoke:

"I need to ask you about something. Could you tell me how's the condition in India?"

Old Man: "I am sorry, Miss Lea, regarding India, as far as I know, it is a dangerous place now to travel, and I recommend not travelling there. Not a single person has returned back after going there."

Lea: "And what about creatures that lurk there? Are they dangerous as the rumours say they are?"

Old Man: "Ah yes, that is true. I am sorry, Miss Lea, I can't recommend you or anyone to go there right now. My own people were devoured by them, and some even became those creatures. I can't let anyone else suffer the same."

Lea: "I understand. Thank you very much."

Lea bowed in gratitude and walked out of the hut, straight to her hut and summoned a bird and tied a small note on the leg of the bird and let it fly away. She went inside and started preparing dinner. She finished preparing dinner and called out to Leo to come for dinner as Lea set the table for dinner. He had just woken up when Lea called out to him and washed his face quickly, and came to the table.

Lea: "How are you feeling now?"

Leo: "I am fine now, mother. Don't worry."

Lea: "I am glad. Sit down, Leo and eat up."

Leo sat and started eating his dinner when he suddenly remembered about the piece in India.

Leo: "Mother."

Lea: "Yes, son."

Leo: "Did you find out anything about India?"

Lea: "Leo, wait till we finish dinner. It's a matter we can't discuss while eating. I will tell you everything after we finish our dinner."

Both of them ate in silence, and when they had finished, Lea took the plates and kept them in the sink to be washed later. She took Leo to the sitting room with her and had him sit down while she sat near him.

Lea: "Leo, listen carefully as to what I am about to tell you. After the radioactive dust entered the atmosphere, many people mutated. In India, there was a different form of mutation. Due to experiments conducted, the mutation changed at a genetic level. They mutated into creatures known as Bone Drainers. As the name implies, they drain the bones of a human body completely. The rest of the body is thrown away. These bone drainers killed the majority of the people living in India. Those who survived hid underground just like we have."

"I have sent a message to certain someone to find out their weakness. Until his message arrives, we need to wait. In the meantime, finish your training. For now, get some sleep."

They both got up, and Lea tugged Leo into the bed and kissed his forehead.

"Leo, get a good sleep. I will see you in the morning, honey."

Leo: "Yes, mother. Good night."

Lea: "Good night, Leo."

Lea extinguished the lamp light nearby and went out of the room, and retired for the night. In the morning, Leo woke up. Though it was hard to tell whether it was morning or night, since they were underground, Leo could assume it was morning as he could hear a lot of buzzes outside. Leo got down from the bed and walked towards his mother, who was busy in the kitchen preparing breakfast.

Leo: "Good morning, mother."

Lea: "Good morning, honey. Had a good sleep?"

Leo: "Yes, mother. Is there anything I can help with?"

Lea: "No, it's alright, Leo. It's almost prepared. Why don't you go and freshen up yourself and sit down at the table?"

Leo: "Yes, mother."

Leo went to freshen up while Lea finished preparing breakfast. Just as she was setting up the table, Leo walked in. They both sat down and had breakfast while he told her about his childhood. After finishing breakfast, she took him to the training ground and she went back after leaving him to train. Leo once again started his training. He closed his minds and cleared his thoughts. The four shadows started to make Leo angry by provoking him. He had to keep his calm along with anger. He kept trying and trying. He would fail and try again. This went on for days and after 1 week he finally got the hang of it.

Next phase came the phase of combat training. He needed to learn both attack and defence. Since they couldn't use their powers to teach him to avoid from letting Kate know, they had been left with the option of physically training him. All of them took turns in training him. The first one had him do some exercises to warm up his body as well as increase his stamina and the duration he could withstand the exhaustion. The second and third trained him in actual combat.

Second Shadow: "Leo, now you have to try to land a hit on me and him. We will be attacking you and you have to defend as well. The basic of any combat training is, you have to be alert and on constant lookout for any attack that can come up from anywhere. Ready?"

After he said this, Leo nodded and the two shadows started attacking him. He was not able to fight at first as he could only try to dodge the attacks. Most of the time he got hit. For few weeks he slowly started to dodge the attacks and avoid from getting hit. Now he had to learn to attack as well while defending. Both shadows attacked him and he successfully dodged them and tried to land a hit on the second shadow but his attack got blocked when he tried to reach one. Weeks passed as he kept on going through rigorous combat training.

In the end, he was able to land attack while defending himself from the two spirits. He had cleared the combat training. Next came the training of the heart. The fourth shadow did nothing of the sort of any exercises or combats. He made him remember the days of his past. The part when he was stabbed with Xeton rods, another where he was almost killed by Kate, many more. This kind of training strengthened his heart. The training went on for months. Final phase was putting all the training together and going up against all the four at once. Almost a year was up and Leo finally finished his training.

Spirit: "Leo, you have completed your training, but awakening your powers will be up to you. We have made you strong physically, and mentally which will help you control your powers, but controlling is up to you. I hope everything goes well. Good Luck."

Leo: "Thank you very much."

Leo bowed and started walking towards the portal. The four spirits disappeared. When suddenly Lea jumped through the portal towards and pushed him along with herself as one of the portals exploded. Lea lay on the ground shielding her son from the explosion. When the explosion ceased, they both got up only to face three cloaked figures. The three cloaked figures were none other than those assassins that Kate had sent to kill Leo.

Lea whispered to herself:

"Impossible. How are they here? They shouldn't be able to find this place. The only ones who can find this place are the Cloudscars or the Assyclops."

She looked at them and spoke: "Why are you here?"

The cloaked figures removed their cloaks and revealed themselves. They had no eyes and noses, just ears. They had no clothes on their upper body. Their body was blood-red in colour with a tattoo of skull pierced with blood dipped blade with two circles encircling it on their stomachs. They were wearing cloth made of fabric which had a shade of black and golden on their lower body with shoe like footwear on their feet. They had no weapons whatsoever. But still, the appearance was way too creepy, giving chills to anyone who laid eyes upon them.

Lea and Leo, too, had chills. She had recognized them.

Lea: "No! there's no way you can be alive. Assyclops were banished from their planet and had become extinct."

Assyclops: "You think so? Hahaha… we survived. If you know us, then you must be one of the Cloudscars. Lady, we came to kill that kid. Stay out of our way if you don't want to be killed."

Lea: "I won't let you harm him. Stay away. Go back where you came from."

Lea turned to Leo and whispered: "Let's retreat, Leo."

They started retreating slowly. But there was no time. Those three figures sprung at them suddenly. The three split off in three different directions, and swords appeared in their hands with skulls embedded on the blades. There were six skulls embedded on it. Lea and Leo were surrounded.

Leo: "Mother, I guess we fight."

Lea: "No other choice. Leo, stay by my side all the time, and we will fight together."

Leo nodded, and those three launched their attacks on them. Lea created a shield around herself and Leo separately to shield them from harm. But as soon as the blades touched those shields, both were thrown off the ground, as the skulls emitted strong pulses. The shield was broken. The next moment one of the Assyclops appeared in front of Leo. It was so sudden that Leo and Lea had no time to react. Out of nowhere, Lea launched herself as a shield in front of Leo to protect him, and the blade touched her body. The skulls send the pulses again, and her body received that attack directly. Her whole body shook with the worst possible pain, and she screamed.

Chapter - 10

DRIFTERS

Part - I

She was thrown due to force of the pulse and landed down on the floor. She was terribly wounded and internally bleeding. She kept on spitting blood as Leo held her in his hands. She touched Leo's cheeks as tears flowed down her cheeks, washing away the bloodstains. Assyclops didn't stop. They again attacked Leo and Lea together. Watching his mother die right in front of his eyes triggered Leo's anger, and he was engulfed with white light. It threw the Assyclops off their feet far away from him and Lea.

Slowly the light dissipated, and Leo was standing on the ground. Only this time, his appearance had changed. He was no longer the Leo he was. He had managed to awaken his dormant powers though he was not able to control them. His face had changed, similar to Jin's. On his upper body, right in the middle, he had a tattoo of ring of stars pierced with two space-coloured blades. On both of his wrist were rings of space-coloured scales. There were four rings of space-coloured scales on each of his arms which was situated at a certain distance apart from each other. Connecting those rings to each other were runes. Those runes were arc-shaped, crisscrossing in between the rings in a helical shape. His hands looked normal.

On his lower body appeared normal black coloured fabric cloth with four rings of wings on each of his legs situated too at a certain distance apart from each other. His feet were covered in bandages, with toes protruding out of the bandages. Leo's presence intimidated those Assyclops. They were too scared to move now. But there was no time to lose, and the middle one sent the other two to attack him while he attacked from behind them. Leo stared at them with fury in his eyes. Four claws like thin rods came out from the space-coloured scales on the wrist on each arm, forming a shape of rugby football with a gap at the end. In the end, a slender long katana shaped sword formed covered in space colour. Those were the nexus blades. In the next moment, Leo just waved those swords, and the bodies of two Assyclops were cut into pieces.

The third Assyclops used his sword to again emit a pulse from a distance. Before Leo could attack further, Lea quickly got up even while she was spitting blood and closed her fingers together in a circle. Everything came to a standstill. Lea had stopped time. She touched Leo and made him move. Leo glared at Lea but found his anger calming down as Lea was casting a warm light which calmed Leo. His appearance started to changed back to his normal self again. Leo caught his mother into his arms and supported her as tears flowed down his cheeks.

Leo: "Mother, please don't push yourself. Let's get out of here."

Lea: "It's too late for me, Leo. Listen, I need to tell you a few things before everything is blown to pieces and I am gone. Don't cry and just listen, honey."

Leo stopped crying and just looked at her silently as tears kept flowing down his cheeks as she continued.

"I have arranged for someone to meet you when you go to the surface from here. Travel to India and retrieve the piece of Eternal. Save Kate and bring her back. Please stay careful always and look after yourself. I.... will.... always.... be.... alive....in.... you."

She had just barely spoken the last line, and she died, enabling the time to move. A light began to grow from Lea's closed fingers, and it exploded, throwing Leo and Assyclops through different portals. Leo was lying face down on the ground, fainted from the explosion and exhaustion while there was no sign of the Assyclops anywhere. It seemed like he had ended up somewhere else. Quite a while passed, and it was almost noon. A cloaked figure walked towards and gently took him into its arms and piggy backed him. The figure walked for a while and entered a cave that was sealed with a barrier. The figure went further and further into the cave and came into an opening where tents were set up.

There beings similar to humans but clad in armour type of clothing. They wore a cyan coloured sleeveless shirt, which was tucked into their cyan coloured pants. On top of the shirt, there were two straps that were wrapped around their shirt and from those straps hung rectangular-shaped patches downward. On their pants were the same straps with just symbols of eyes on them. There were three straps on each side of the pants at an equal distance apart from each other. At the back of their shirt was a symbol of a shield in the form of rounded edged triangle. Three snake heads were visible situated almost near edge of the shield. A single snake at the center.

Everyone watched the figure as it took Leo straight up to a tent. The figure entered the tent and placed Leo on the bed there. Another figure came in and spoke:

"Is this him? It looks like he has been through a lot."

The cloaked figure removed the cloak and revealed itself. The figure was none other than Rose herself. She turned to the other figure and spoke:

"Yes, Asti. He is Leo, the one you have been waiting for. Let him rest for now. Let's go out. (Turning towards the entrance she called:) Rea, Nei."

Two girls came into the tent. Rose spoke to them:

"Take care of him until I am back."

Rose went out, leaving Leo in those girls' hands. Meanwhile, on the marble ring in Ranxus,

Kate was standing on the ring waiting for the news of Leo's death. A Xerker came in behind her and spoke:

"My queen."

Kate: "What's the news, Gare?"

Gare: “The news is bad. The Assyclops that were sent to kill Leo are dead. Leo is injured but still alive. Though he has disappeared, we can’t trace him. Also, Lea is dead. She died protecting Leo.”

Kate: “The Assyclops failed, huh (Kate was furious). It looks like we will have to race it out with Leo to India. Bring Has and Kal. I want to talk with them.”

Gare: “Yes, my queen.”

Gare retreated to bring those two Xerkers while Kate started thinking. After a few minutes, Gare brought Has and Kal to Kate and left them. She turned towards those two and spoke:

“It’s time, you two. Pack yourselves. We will be travelling to India tomorrow. I have found where the piece is. This time it will be a battle between Leo and us. Let’s kill him this time. Go ahead and make preparations. Has and Kal both spoke in one voice:

“Yes, my queen.”

They retreated, leaving Kate alone. Meanwhile,

Leo woke up suddenly to find himself in the tent with the two girls Rose had left behind to take care of him. Clutching his head as it was hurting very much, he tried to get up but felt weak. He fell back onto the bed. The girls went to hold Leo. He looked at them and asked:

“Who are you? Where am I?”

Rea: “Calm down, no need to panic. I am Rea, and she is Nei. We were told to take care of you by Lady Rose. You should lie and take a rest. You were badly wounded, so we put ointments on your wounds. Let them heal up first. Lady Rose is out at the moment. When she comes back, she will tell you everything."

Leo: "Rose? Is she the same Rose from Ranxus?"

Rea: "Yes, she is. Please rest for now. When she comes back, we will let her know."

Leo was already tired and weak, and it didn't take long for him to fall asleep. After a while, Rose came back. Rea and Nei told her everything. Rose asked them to go out and let her be alone with him. After they both went out, Rose sat down beside Leo and caressed his forehead gently and whispered:

"I am sorry, Leo, you had to go through much."

Leo started to wake up slowly, feeling Rose's touch. His eyes weren't wide open, but he felt the warm touch, just like his mother. He whispered:

"Mother, is that you?"

Rose: "Leo, just rest for now. Let's talk when you are all well and healed up. Good night, Leo."

Leo: "Good night, mother."

Rose kissed his forehead as he fell back asleep. She got up quietly and walked out of the tent, where she was met by Asti.

Asti: "Lady Rose, the message from Shyam has arrived."

Rose: "Good. I have been waiting for that. Let's go."

They both walked towards another tent. The next morning, Leo woke refreshed and completely healed up. He sat up on the bed and looked around. It was a normal tent with a huge bed in the center on which he lay. Around it was fire stands with gaps between them. There were two chairs and a table a certain distance away from the bed. Straight away from the bed in which Leo was sitting, he saw a curtain which was the entrance to the tent. Just then, Rose entered the tent and was happy to see Leo. Leo got up and ran into Rose's open arms. Leo was crying as he hugged Rose. Rose sensed something had to happened to Lady Lea, so she just patted gently on his back.

Rose: "It's alright, Leo. Let it all out. You are safe with me. She will always be by your side. And remember, she is always alive inside your heart."

Leo: "It's all my fault that she died. If she hadn't protected me, she would still be alive."

Rose: "Leo, listen. She died protecting you because she wanted you to live on. You need to save Kate and everyone else. You are everyone's hope and make sure Lady Lea didn't die in vain. When she died, she left her feelings deep inside your heart. So, whenever you feel down, just close your eyes and you will be able to feel and see her. You need to stay strong Leo."

Leo cried till he was able to calm down and looked at Rose.

Rose: "That's better, Leo. Let's eat something first."

As Leo was washing his face in the water, at that next moment, food was brought to them by the same two girls who took care of Leo. They both sat down at the table and started eating while those two girls left them.

Rose: "Leo, could you please tell me what happened in there?"

Leo: "Yes."

Leo explained everything. On how the Assyclops found them and Lea sacrificed herself to protect him and how he turned into another being, and he couldn't remember after that not until he was kneeling down near his dying mother. Rose kind of turned serious when she heard he had awakened his powers.

Rose: "I am sorry to hear that, Leo. Hope her soul can rest in peace.

Leo: "I wish I could have done something to protect her that time and had been in control of my powers."

Rose: "Leo, you did protect her you know. You defeated those assassins when you awakened the powers inside you. But you couldn't control because you were completely absorbed by your rage. It's alright."

Leo: "Thank you Rose. When I awakened those powers, something felt different and energetic. My blood boiled and I felt I was going to split apart.

Rose: "It's normal to feel like that when you awaken your powers the first time. And now you can easily awaken them anytime. You just have to follow what you were taught by those spirits, and train to control it. You just have to think back to the feeling you had those powers and make yourself stronger. You try that while you remain here for the time being."

Chapter - 11

DRIFTERS

Part - II

After they had finished their breakfast, they both walked out of the tent. As they were walking along the path between the tents, many pairs of eyes stared towards Leo. He felt uncomfortable. He quickly started a conversation with Rose.

Leo: "Rose, what happened to you and everyone else? Where are Jin and the others? And who are these people?"

Rose: "I don't know. We got separated due to the explosion. So, I don't know what happened to them. I was injured and lying among the rubbles of a house nearby when these beings found me and brought me here. I have been here since then. Slowly I got in touch with Lady Lea even before she found you. Regarding the beings you see, they are called Drifters. Drifters are those beings who are experts in using weapons. They are also known as Weapon Masters."

Leo: "What's that symbol on their shirts?"

Just as Leo had finished his question, Asti came near them. Rose signalled Asti to wait. Asti bowed and stopped in his tracks and backed up a bit as rose explained:

"That symbol is the zodiac of Death Sizzler, the star of their planet. A death sizzler is a snake that will look short in length, but it can expand and contract its skin according to its prey. Its upper body's scales turn into blades that can cut its prey's body into pieces so that the snake can easily swallow its prey. It can also kill its prey without any efforts as it can throw its scales as blades and cut of the body's essential parts and make it handicapped and unable to fight back. Its skin is very tough and is not easy to kill"

Leo: "Woah, sounds cool and dangerous."

Rose smiled as she indicated Asti to come forward and tell them.

Asti: "He is waiting."

Rose nodded and continued:

"Come with me, Leo. I need you to meet someone."

Rose walked towards a tent nearby, followed by Leo and Asti. They entered inside the tent where a human was sitting there. The human had a brownish kind of colour to his skin.

Rose: "Leo, meet Shyam. He is from India. And he is the one to whom your mother had sent the message."

Leo: "Hello. Nice to meet you."

Leo extended his hand for a handshake, but Shyam just enclosed his hands as done in Indian tradition and said namaste. Leo copied him and did the same.

Shyam: "It's an honour to meet you, master Leo"

Leo smiled and said:

"The honour is mine."

Rose: "I am sorry to interrupt but time is not on our side as Kate is putting her plans in motion as we speak. Mr. Shyam if you will please."

Shyam nodded his head and spoke:

"I was saved by your mother when I was running away from those monsters in India. She took me to a nearby town and helped me find a home. I am indebted to your mother. She sent me a message asking me about the situation in India. Since I couldn't send a message back to her, I came here to personally tell you. Listen, carefully."

"The condition in India is very bad. Almost all of the underground villages have crumbled. Only one village remains in Central India. I used to live there. We used to send a few people up to the surface every day to salvage food."

Leo: "Food? Wasn't everything destroyed when nuclear blasts occurred?

Shyam: "No, Leo. You see, India had turned into a powerful nation with advanced technologies. So, they had created a barrier using nanomachines and protected many cities from the blast. But due to genetic experiments conducted on the mutated people from the affected cities, everything changed. The creatures called bone drainers destroyed cities and killed many people and ate them as their food source was the bones inside our body."

"People who survived moved to underground cities which were built over time. Since bone drainers can't eat human food, the stores were left alone, and it slowly got covered with moss. Due to a lack of human food, bone drainers preyed upon each other, and they further mutated. But the trouble didn't end there. The food we had managed to store up in the underground cities dried up not long ago. People started resurfacing, and this made them an easy target for bone drainers. Slowly and slowly thousands of people died until only our city was left underground."

"Then, one day, I was sent to the surface along with others. We had no other option left as farming underground wasn't easy. There were four of us. We went to a nearby store. We had managed to salvage enough food to take back with us. We pushed the food in wheel carts slowly without making sounds when one of our member's wheel carts slipped and fell to the ground. Just then, a bone drainer which was lying nearby popped up and came running at us."

"They have no face. Those creatures have one mouth on their upper body in a triangular shape, which can split up into three mouths. They are fast. They have additional three feet on each leg with ears just above their feet. They were way too scary, and the noise they make will give you ear-splitting pain. They ran after us as we dashed up to the manhole which led to the underground city. I was in the front with the other three behind my back. Just then, I heard a scream, as one of the members had been caught."

"The bone drainer just sucked out his bones through his neck even when he was alive. It was a horrific site; I cannot explain more of it. We just had reached the manhole cover and lifted it up when two other bone drainers popped up out of nowhere and caught the other two behind me. The carts that we had in our hands fell down the manhole into the city. I quickly climbed into the manhole and down the ladder and retreated back into the city fast. But what I thought to be my town was just another abandoned town."

"For days, I stayed there salvaging whatever food was available. Days and weeks passed by until one day I heard a noise not far from where I lay. I took hold of a rusted weapon. I waited in silence, praying it wasn't a bone drainer. Then suddenly, a cloaked figure came in to view and stopped me from hitting her with the weapon. That person was your mother. Since then, I have been a good friend of her."

Leo: "How did my mother even find you? How did she get past all the bone drainers?"

Shyam: "Alas, I don't know how but she had come there in the search of something called piece of Eternal. While she was searching for it, she found me."

Shyam touched Leo's shoulder and spoke sympathetically:

"I am sorry for your loss Leo. She was a very good woman."

Leo smiled and nodded his head in agreement. For a minute, no one spoke. Rose finally broke the silence:

"Mr. Shyam, could you please tell us the weakness of those creatures and how to get past them. We need to get to the loophole."

Shyam: "Ah, the loophole. I will tell you everything I know. The bone drainers attacked people based on vibrations you create. Even the tiniest of vibration can be heard, but they can't make out your location with a tiny vibration. Just be careful that you don't make big vibrations. Stay in the shadows. And they can't travel underground as in the dark they cannot hear."

"Though I will be accompanying you along the way, please remember what I told you. When do you want to go?"

Rose: "I was thinking, tomorrow morning itself. The ones that will go are Leo, myself and you. Rest all will be here, and they know what to do in case things got worse here. Thank you, Mr. Shyam, for telling us everything. I will take your leave. Leo and I have something to talk about in private. Thank you very much."

Shyam smiled and bowed his head as Leo and Rose bowed their heads and moved out of the tent and went back to her tent. Rose beckoned no one except Leo to follow her, and they both went inside. Rose looked at Leo and spoke:

"Leo, are you sure the piece is there in the loophole?"

Leo: "Yes, Rose. I am sure. I heard it from Eternal herself."

Rose: "Alright, Leo. Listen, tomorrow, whatever happens, remember never to look back and keep running. This time no one else is there to save us. And there is a chance we might bump into Lady Kate. So just hold on to your anger and do not act recklessly."

Leo: "Ok, Rose, I won't act recklessly."

Rose: "Alright, Leo. Time to sleep. You will be sleeping in the tent next to mine. I will wake you up in the morning. Right now, it's time for dinner with everyone. Come, let's go."

Rose led Leo to a dining hall nearby. It was a giant cave just situated at the end of the path. As they entered the cave, Leo saw there lots of circular shaped balls inside a glass lamp. They emitted bright white light on the path of the cave. They continued on the path until they reached an opening and entered the dining hall. It was just like an old human-made dining hall with wooden benches and tables and cooks serving food to everyone. Some were dancing around, some singing and others eating food and drinking. After quite a while, everyone retired for the night while Leo and Rose separated and went to their tents. The next morning, Nei came to wake Leo and gave him the clothes. She told him to get ready soon as Rose was waiting for him.

Nei went away as Leo washed up and got ready. The clothes he wore were different from those drifters. The clothes had the same colour, but at the back of the sleeveless shirt, there was the symbol of Ranxus, the same one that was on Jin's back. On the pants, on both sides, was a space-coloured strap helically wound from top to bottom. On one side was the moon, and on the other side was the sun. In the front of his shirt was, two circles of stars crisscrossed to each other. Two blood-coloured blades pierced those stars, and the blades were also crisscrossed. He wore the clothes. He was also wearing normal elbow bands that covered his elbow area. He walked out of his tent towards Rose's tent. He had become quite handsome.

Few girls who were drifters kept smiling and whispering themselves while looking at him. Leo entered Rose's tent and saw her waiting there. She was wearing the same clothes on the day he met her. Rose saw him and blushed while looking at him and spoke:

"Leo, you look very handsome in those clothes. Do those clothes fit you properly?"

Leo: "Thank you, you look beautiful too. Yes, they perfectly match."

Rose: "Thank you too, Leo. I am glad they fit. These clothes were made by your mother for you. She gave them to me just in case something happened to her. Let's go."

Rose and Leo walked out of the tent to the dining hall. Shyam was waiting at the door for them. He was dressed in the same clothing as drifters. They went inside and had breakfast. Later those three said their goodbyes and Leo thanked everyone for taking care of him. They set out wearing a cloak and a mask to protect themselves from the outside atmosphere.

Chapter - 12

BONE DRAINERS

Part - I

Leo: "Rose, where are we exactly?"

Rose: "Leo, we are currently what used to be France or what's left of it now."

Rose took out a device and pressed a button on the side, and a holographic map appeared. Since most of the technology had been destroyed by the Xerkers so very few things were available, including the map device. Rose conferred with Shyam, and he nodded and let them through. They walked through the rubbles, crossing cities one by one. It was a long walk. They would rest at night and in the morning start walking again. A horse would have been better in this situation, was Leo's thinking. But he knew that all animals had become extinct now since everything, including those precious cities, were destroyed.

It was nightfall when they stopped. They had almost reached the border of France. They sat down inside a broken-down house, and they together set up a tent. It was quite spacious with a separate bathroom cum toilet. The tent protected them from the outside atmosphere. They took off their cloaks and masks as Rose started cooking dinner along with Shyam. After having food, they all fell asleep. Around midnight, Leo woke up from a nightmare. He got up and wore the mask and cloak, and went outside.

Leo sat down at the broken wall nearby, staring at the almost visible night sky. Very few stars were visible now. The radioactive dust had somehow settled into the clouds making the air harmless as it should have been and the sky was slightly visible now in some parts of the planet while other parts did need cloaks and masks. After quite a while, Rose came as she had woken up feeling thirsty and seeing Leo gone, she came out worried. She saw him and sat near him. Leo was suddenly surprised to see her as she made no sound when she came near him.

Leo: "You need to stop sneaking up on me every time."

Rose: "It's kind of fun. You know I used to do it every time during our childhood. Scaredy cat."

Leo: "Alright, alright. I am not a scaredy-cat."

Rose: "Hahahaha. Anyway, Leo, what are you doing outside?"

Leo looked at Rose and spoke:

"I had a dream where I saw sis destroying everything, and the stars fell onto the ground burning everything they touched."

Rose: “Leo, it’s just a dream, and you know we can stop it. That’s why we are going in search of the piece of Eternal.”

Leo: “What if I fail to save this planet? What if I lose you, my sis and everyone else?”

Rose: “Leo, it’s not in our hands to determine how anyone should live or die. But it’s in our hands to show them a new path. So just remember, no matter what, I will always be by your side. Come on now, let’s get some sleep.”

Rose extended out her hand towards Leo after she got up.

Leo: “Thank you, Rose.”

Leo took her hand and got up. He looked at her and smiled and spoke:

“Rose, do you remember how we used to lie down on the soft grass and gaze at the stars for hours. I wish those days would come back.”

Rose: “Leo, those days cannot be brought back but let’s gaze at the stars again when everything is over.”

Leo: “Promise Rose?”

Rose: “Promise.”

Both of them smiled at each other.

Rose: “Come on. Let’s go now. We need to be up early.”

They both went inside and fell asleep. The next morning, they packed everything and continued their journey. Since they didn’t feel the hunger in the current atmosphere, so they didn’t stop to eat for lunch and just ate breakfast and dinner. This went on for days. Walking and resting at times. Slowly as days passed, Rose and Leo grew closer to each other as they hung out and talked to each other. Finally, falling in love. They had almost reached the borders of India. That night they camped just a few miles away from the Indian border in an abandoned house that was still standing. The air inside the house was breathable as the air breather was still working. As usual, Leo and Rose were sitting outside close to each other.

Rose: "Leo, tomorrow we get inside the Indian border. No matter what happens, just stay close to me, and I will protect you from any harm."

Rose spoke those words with a smile, but Leo knew she was scared inside as her shaking hands gave her away. Leo held her hands and looked at her and spoke:

"Rose, it's alright. I will never leave your side. I will be watching your back, so just relax."

Rose calmed down, listening to the gentle voice of Leo. As the night deepened, they both stared at each other's eyes, deepening the eye contact. Slowly their heads came closer to each other, and their nose touched each other, and their lips touched each other. They kissed. It was a long and passionate kiss. After quite a while, they broke apart, blushing. They went back to sleep smiling and blushing. The next morning, they reached the Indian border, but they stopped in their tracks. Leo and Rose were surprised to see a huge wall just in front of them. It was around 50 feet high or more.

Shyam: "It's to keep those monsters inside. It was built by the United Nations. Don't worry, I know a door somewhere nearby that can get us inside. Just wait here."

Shyam went forward to search for the passage leaving Rose and Leo. After quite a while, Shyam came back and asked them to follow him. They walked not very far from the spot. They arrived at the door. Shyam held Leo's hands, and Leo held Rose's as Shyam pressed his hand on the door, and the door just disappeared, revealing a passage. They went inside, and the door disappeared.

Shyam: "Currently, we are standing in what used to be Jammu and Kashmir. This way, let's go."

Shyam led them through the dry land. They walked on for a couple of hours when they reached a fence which had broken board on it on which danger was written. Shyam turned to both of them and spoke:

"This is where the dangerous path starts. Stick to the shadows and make no noise and move with silence. No fires too. Just stay with me, and if anything happens, then just run. Let's go."

They started walking. Since there were rubbles, they used to carefully hide and walk. This continued for many days, but there was no sign of any bone drainer anywhere, not until they arrived in Delhi. Just as they neared the Delhi border, a bone drainer came in to view. It was resting near the rubble. All three of them quietly walked past the creature in the shadows that was exhibited due to torn down multi-storeyed buildings, though all of them seem on the verge of crumbling down any second.

Suddenly Shyam directed them with his hand to stop. Another bone drainer had popped up in the view. It had become dangerous. Shyam signalled them using his hands to go back another way. So, they slowly retreated. Just then, accidentally, Leo knocked off a rod that was hanging off the window, and the clanking sound of metal on the ground not only woke the sleeping bone drainer but alerted the other one who had just popped up. Now both creatures awake and on alert, they had to be careful not to get caught.

They kept retreating back when suddenly a gust of wind blew, making the building shake a bit, and walls started crumbling down on the ground. Those three had no choice but to run. So, they broke into a run, following Shyam towards another building. The creatures noticed their movement and ran after them at a fast pace. Their three feet made them fast while chasing their prey. Three of them went inside a nearby building. It was not completely dark but still hidable.

They hid behind the wall in the shadows trying to catch their breath as they heard footsteps echoing nearer and nearer. Suddenly the sound stopped, and all they could hear was the clanking of metals and bricks onto the ground. When the sound died out for a split second, they had a sigh of relief, thinking they were safe, when next moment, an ear-splitting noise echoed. It was the noise made by bone drainers to make their prey unable to move. The noise they generated acted as sonar sounds, too, which could tell the location of their prey.

Those three endured the pain and just hid from those creatures waiting for them to go away. Those creatures kept on making noises until it was dark and since they couldn't find anything, they gave up. For quite a while, they waited, and when they saw no sign of those creatures, they decided it was time to move. All three of them got up and walked out of the building into the moonlight. It was a full moon that night. With the fear of those creatures who could be lurking around, they moved cautiously. They just had crossed two buildings when they found their path blocked by a bone drainer. It looked the same way as Shyam had described to them.

Closely seeing the creature was scarier than hearing about it in the stories. They tried to retreat but found another bone drainer blocking their path. They turned in another direction and found the third one. They had been ambushed. It was a very difficult situation that they were in. Shyam turned around and looked at Leo and Rose and whispered:

"I am sorry, there is no other choice. I will distract them while both of you run. There is an underground tunnel nearby, which will take you to safety. Hide in that tunnel, and these creatures won't get you when there is no light. On the count of three."

Leo: No, you can't."

Leo wanted to protest against the idea, but Rose stopped him by placing her hand on Leo's shoulder and indicating that was the only way as bone drainers are tough to be killed. Battling three right now would be dangerous as it would make other bone drainers gather here.

Shyam: "Sorry, it's the only way."

Rose: "Thank you for helping us get this far. May you find peace."

Chapter - 13

BONE DRAINERS

Part - II

The next moment Shyam made a run between the bone drainers towards the open area, while Leo and Rose made a dash for it as those bone drainers ran towards Shyam. Rose and Leo reached an old manhole cover and slid it open. As they were entering the tunnel, that's when they heard Shyam's scream, which died out after a few seconds. Shyam had died at the hands of those creatures. They both entered the underground tunnel and waited till morning. The next morning, Rose went up the tunnel towards the surface to see if they had left. There was no sign of those creatures. Assuming them to have left, Rose signalled Leo to come out silently. They both walked away without making a noise towards the underground city in Central India. For days they walked and hid whenever they saw a bone drainer nearby.

Finally, they had reached central India following the map. But the entrance to the city was nowhere to be found. No matter how much they searched, they didn't find one. Just when they had given hope, they found themselves surrounded by those creatures again, and this time there were six of them. It was spelt doom for them. Both of them froze on the spot with hands held together when all of a sudden, smoke cans were thrown on those creatures creating a time frame for Leo and Rose to escape. Through the smoke, they saw the light not far away from them.

Leo and Rose dashed for it. Because of the smoke, the footsteps echoed everywhere, and bone drainers were confused. Leo and Rose came across a person who was an Indian. He indicated them to climb down the ladder and into the city. They both quickly climbed down as the man shut the hole with the lid. All three of them climbed for quite some time before stepping on the ground. They had finally arrived at the city Shyam spoke off.

After finally landing on the ground, the person looked towards Leo and Rose. In the next moment, they were surrounded by a lot of Indians with spears. The person finally spoke:

"What business do you have here? Who are you?"

Rose: "Before we speak, shouldn't you be the first to introduce?"

The person smirked at her response and spoke:

"I commend your boldness, woman. But you are our prisoner now. So, tell us who you are."

Rose didn't want to fight, so she spoke:

"I am Rose, and this is Leo. We were with an Indian named Shyam who hailed from this town. We are just on our way to the loophole."

The person looked at Rose and again asked:

"Where is Shyam?"

Rose: "Unfortunately, he sacrificed himself to help us both escape. I am sorry."

The person sighed and spoke:

"Alas, he always did that. Sacrificing himself for others. I am Shyam's brother Nitin. Nice to meet you, Lady Rose and Lord Leo. (seeing their surprised faces) I am sorry we didn't recognize you. Welcome here. Please follow me. I would like you to meet someone."

Rose nodded and indicated Leo to stay close to her, and they both followed Nitin while all the others followed them behind. There were lots of houses. All of the houses were made of wood since there was no bricks or cement available. Nitin, Rose and Leo walked straight to a house just situated in front, while others broke off to their respective posts. They entered the house through a wooden door. Inside the house, everything was made of wood and well-polished. It shined in the light. There in the main hall, a man was sitting in the chair while a few others stood around him discussing something. That man seemed to be the leader there. He looked at Leo and Rose and got up and spoke:

"Welcome to the city Lady Rose. I am Vicky. May I know who the young man is?"

Rose: "Sir, this is Leo, the Wingblade."

Vicky: "Ah, Lord Leo. Welcome to the city. Nice to meet you both."

Vicky bowed to them, and they bowed back in return.

Vicky: "What brings you two here?"

Rose: "We are here looking for the loophole."

Vicky: "Ah, the loophole. I would suggest you ask Dr Ruchi. She knows about it more than any of us. She is the one who studied it and sealed it. Nitin here will take care of your needs and look after both of you. Meanwhile, let me finish my work and will join you."

Rose: "Thank you."

Rose and Leo bowed and walked after Nitin. He led them straight to a shop nearby for food, and later, he took them to Dr Ruchi's place. They sat down with her while Nitin went off, leaving them alone to talk. Rose explained everything in detail to Dr Ruchi. After hearing everything, she stood up and walked to a desk nearby and took out an old map. She brought it to them and set it on the table as she sat down and spoke:

"The place you seek is right here. (pointing to the location on the map). But there is a slight problem."

Rose: "What's wrong?"

Ruchi: "This location is right in the middle of bone drainer's nest. I was one of the doctors involved in illegal genetic research conducted secretly on mutated humans. When the first loophole came here, strange beings emerged from it who killed many people living near it. So, our military used the firepower to bring them, and the few of them retreated, and few of them were killed."

"The dead bodies of those beings were used for genetic experiments on mutated humans. That's how bone drainers were born. The laboratory was completely wiped out. I escaped as I was on holiday that day. But before I left, I had secretly cast an electromagnetic pulse net over the loophole to prevent anything from coming out. I don't know if it's still there. Ever since the laboratory was destroyed, I was never able to track it. What do you two seek there?"

Rose: "We are looking for the piece of Eternal, and we got a message it was in the loophole. Do you know anything regarding that?"

Ruchi: "Ah, alas, I don't know. But I do remember seeing a shining rune blade in the hands of a being who retreated back into the loophole. I guess that's the thing you have been looking for. I can show you the way, but I won't stay for long. I will leave you and come back. Sorry, I can't face those creatures."

Rose: "It's alright. We understand. So, when do we go?"

Ruchi: "Let's go at dawn tomorrow. For now, you should rest. It must have been a tiring journey for you. I will see you in the morning. Nitin here (who had just popped into view) will take you to your place of stay. See you then."

Leo and Rose stood up and walked behind Nitin towards the door and Leo stopped in his and looked back at Ruchi and spoke:

"You have delicious food here. How do you get the ingredients to make them so delicious?"

Ruchi: "We salvage old grocery stores on the surface when possible and we also grow the ingredients on our farms underground."

Leo: "Underground farming? I thought it was not possible due to terrain disadvantages."

Ruchi: "We developed our own artificial farming methods. That's how we are able to provide our city with food sources."

Leo: "Ah, I see. Thank you for telling me."

Ruchi: "My pleasure."

Nitin took them to a house which was kept for guests only if any ventured here. They retired for the night after having dinner. The next morning, Ruchi was right there at the door, all ready to move. Rose, Leo and Ruchi had breakfast together and set out on the journey.

Ruchi: "We won't be going through the surface as it's too dangerous. Instead, we will be taking an abandoned underground tunnel that connects this place to that location. It was used for transferring materials a long time ago."

This time all three of them walked in another direction opposite to the one they had come. They climbed a few boulders and reached the tunnel entrance. It was dark. Ruchi led them through the tunnel right up to the location. She quietly removed the manhole cover and peeped outside.

Ruchi: "There seems to be no sign of them. Come on, let's go."

Three of them silently stepped onto the surface. They walked in silence and suddenly came to a halt. Right in front was the laboratory of Dr Ruchi, and right at the entrance of the laboratory lay a bone drainer.

Ruchi: "Ok. Listen. Here is the plan."

Ruchi whispered something to Rose and Leo and left them and went forward while Rose and Leo hid near the building. Rose went to the right side of her lab and opened a lid on the wall, and pressed the button inside. At once, a huge explosion occurred some distance away. The bone drainers inhabiting the lab quickly ran towards the explosion. Ruchi had set explosives a few kilometres away from the lab just in case. Thankfully they had been still active. Ruchi then indicated Rose and Leo to enter the lab. Another surprise waited for them inside the lab. The net had been broken down as if slashed by something and the loophole was active though no one came out of it.

Ruchi: "Seems like someone or something destroyed the net. Luckily no creature has come out, which is way too strange. Well, there is the loophole. (turning to Rose and Leo) are you both sure that you want to go through?"

Rose: "Yes. Thank you for your help. We will take it from here."

Ruchi: "Alright, I understand. It's been my pleasure helping you. Be safe and be careful. You don't know what to expect. I will be going back to the city before those bone drainers return. Good luck."

Ruchi left them and quickly retreated. Rose and Leo took a deep breath and looked at each other, and jumped into the portal without wasting time.

Chapter – 14

FOUR LEGIONS

The next moment they both stepped onto something hard. They both had landed on a ground which was red in colour with no grass on it. There were huge rocks made of space that lay on the ground, and a wide trench was covering the ground around the rocks. A solid black coarse liquid was flowing from those rocks on the ground into the trench. Those rocks were situated randomly. They both barely had time to rest when out of nowhere, strange beings appeared.

One had runes all over her face. She had three eyes on each side which were in the shape of a triangle. In the center of each triangle was a nose. She had a normal mouth. She was wearing a redshirt over which she wore a banner type of cloth which lay on her body, and she had red scaled pants on. There was a belt on top of the banner clothing at the waist. Lines were extending from the runes on her through her neck, and it went down towards her hands and formed a circle on her wrist.

She had claws for hands with sharp nails. She had a tail that was H-shaped at the end. Her feet were also like claws with sharp toenails. She grinned at the sight of Leo showing her fangs. Rose held Leo's hand tightly when the girl grinned at Leo. Seeing her, the girl also grinned at Rose. Another being had no hands. He had the same clothes on him. His face was different, though. He had slits in his eyes which seemed like nose and eyes together. He had two mouths. One mouth on each side of the cheek. His legs seemed normal like any human. There were two more beings though one of them had features just like the girl, and the other girl had the same feature similar to that guy.

Strange glue-like strips came out of that guy's body and attached to Rose and Leo, and wrapped around them. Rose and Leo couldn't move as they felt themselves weakening. The guy spoke:

"Well, well. We have caught ourselves with quite a fair play. Queen Kien will certainly, be pleased."

Rose and Leo were taken down the path. The guy at the back while the three girls formed a triangle around Rose and Leo. The girl who grinned at Leo kept tracing her hands across his face and shoulder, which made Leo quite uncomfortable while Rose was getting furious. But she couldn't do anything as she felt weak and could hardly make up the strength to walk. After walking for quite a while, they saw what seemed to be a big structure in the shape of a 3D square.

There were four walls that formed the structure. The walls were situated at four corners of the structure, while a semi-transparent material covered the walls. The top of the corners extended diagonally, slanting upwards where they met at the center to form a roof. The was a single entrance in front to go in and out, and guards were standing whose appearance was similar to their captors.

There are many structures like that. As they walked through the path past the structures, the guards gave them looks as if they had made a mistake coming here. Rose and Leo were taken straight to a similar structure and taken inside. Inside the structure, straight at the end were two chairs with a woman and a man sitting on them. She had the same features as that of the girl with the tail. And the man had the same features as that of the guy holding Leo and Rose. Guards were standing on both sides with torches burning around the area with their legs buried into the ground.

Rose and Leo were taken before the woman and man. The girl in front bowed her head and spoke:

"We found these two beside the portal. They are both quite a fine play for the tournament, your highnesses."

The woman got up and came near Rose and Leo and stared at them for quite a while, making circles around them. She spoke finally in a trancing voice:

"Indeed, they seem to be. Tell me, who are you both? And why are you here for?"

Rose knew hiding the truth was a waste, so she spoke with a daring voice:

"I am Rose, a Cloudscar from Ranxus. This boy is Leo, the King of Ranxus. We have come here to get the piece of

Eternal. Let us go and help us get the piece, and we will forget this ever happened."

The woman laughed while the man stood there sad. The woman spoke:

"I don't care whether you are a king or not. Here you are just commoners now and my prisoners. You both would be quite a sport for the tournament. Take them and throw them in with the others."

Both of them were taken towards another arc (3d square structure) where they were put in with other prisoners. In Rose and Leo's arc, five other humans were chained up. Rose and Leo were also chained up. While three of them went away, the girl who took fancy on Leo stayed near him and traced her fingers again on his cheeks and then licked his right cheek, which made Leo uncomfortable. She smiled and then walked away as Rose scorned at her.

Later that night, when everyone was sleeping, the girl snuck into the arc again and came near Leo, who lay on the ground. Rose was just beside him. She crept up near him without making a noise and bent down near him and smelled him. She then traced her fingers again on his face and this time on his lips. Leo opened his eyes due to uneasiness and saw the girl and tried to scream, but the girl covered his mouth and quickly stung her tail onto Leo, which made him unable to move his hands and feet and unable to speak. This time she had Leo completely to herself.

She removed her hand and bent closer to his face, close enough that Leo could feel her breath on him. Then she whispered to him:

"You are quite a fancy boy, Leo. No wonder I fell in love with you at first sight. Come on, Leo, marry me, and I will make you stand above these prisoners. I don't want to see you suffer."

Leo moved his eyes indicating no. That's when she didn't say anything more and kissed his lips right away. She stuck her tongue inside his mouth and started playing with his tongue. It was such a hot and passionate kiss that she didn't realize when she accidentally knocked Rose with her elbow. Rose woke up and saw the girl kissing Leo in front of her. She was furious and shouted:

"Get off him, girl. He is mine."

Rose kind of raised her leg to push her away, but she had already broken off and run off. Due to the ruckus, everyone in the arc woke up, and the guards arrived. Rose just told them she just woke up from a dream. The guards went back to their post. Rose looked at Leo angrily as if ready to smack his head. Meanwhile, the effect left on Leo by the girl seemed to have gone. Leo started to move a bit.

Rose: "How could you let her kiss you?"

Leo: "Rose, calm down. I was paralyzed by her. I couldn't move."

Rose was staring at Leo furiously, which sent shivers down Leo's spine. While others who lay in the tent also felt the chills.

Rose: "Wait, did she attack you with the tail?"

Leo: "Yes, why?"

Rose took a deep sigh and spoke:

"Leo, I had a hunch, but now it's confirmed. She has something to do with space dragons."

Leo: "Space Dragons. Like the actual dragons? Really?"

Rose: "Yes."

Rose turned around just in time and caught the others taking a peek. As soon as their eyes met, those five quickly closed their eyes as if nothing had happened. At this point, Rose was scary even for Leo to handle. Rose quickly spoke:

"Hey guys, I need to talk with you."

They started nudging each other to get up. After quite a while, one of them got up shaking and came near them. His hands were also tied up. Rose asked him to sit down, and he sat with a scared look.

Rose: "Sorry for scaring you. I need to know what's going on here?"

The man slowly started calming down as Rose had begun to show normality around her. The man spoke:

"This place is the planet of four legions. The only planet in the solar system. The four legions consisted of Stickers, Hasters, Neckets and..."

Rose: "Space Dragons, right?"

The man nodded. Rose seemed to have lost in thought as her eyes wandered from the man towards the entrance. Leo looked at Rose and asked:

"Rose, what's wrong?"

Rose: "Leo, this was a prosperous planet a long time ago. Even before Eraser was released."

"The four legions were the four races who were as powerful as us Cloudscars. Then the day came when the earth started crumbling, and this loophole opened. Many beings from here came to our lands to explore and slaughtered many Indians. A war broke out towards the survival of Indians. We intervened and stopped the attack. When the peace was restored, and the beings were pushed back into the loophole, the four of us temporarily used our powers to close off the loophole and meanwhile, the Indian government started working out on how to seal the loophole permanently."

The man nodded and spoke:

"That's when I was brought here along with Dr Ruchi. I am Dr Hari. We both worked together on the loophole. Mainly I was assigned to genetic experiments. That's where we went wrong, and we created the bone drainers. Since you are here, you already know the condition outside. Our lab was the nest for them I with my colleagues jumped into the loophole and ended up here to escape those monsters. The loophole was not only opened here. The disturbance in the energy flow of the universe was so devastating that loopholes like this one opened on other planets too."

"As we escaped into the loophole, we sealed it using the emp net. When we came here, that's when we learned that meanwhile, some beings had ventured on to our land, the piece of Eternal had fallen into the hands of the beings from the loophole and they took it back, and everything turned to ruin the moment piece of Eternal landed upon the planet of the four legions. Each legion wanted their claim on it, and thus war broke out between the four legions. But some didn't want war and stayed away. We helped those beings escape to planet earth. I don't know what happened to them."

Rose: "They were given a place to stay at Ruzone, one of the twin kingdoms to help control the evil side of the core."

The man nodded and spoke:

"Oh, that's a relief. Now back to where I was."

"In short, two legions sided together to destroy the other two legions. The fight continued for many days. Resources got destroyed, millions died. Finally, space dragons and stickers survived and annihilated the others. Though they survived, their losses were huge in number, not to mention the natural resources that went extinct. Many years passed. The planet healed itself slowly as the core of that planet had that capability to self-regenerate though it was a slow process."

Chapter – 15

LEGIONS TOURNAMENT – REVOLVING BLADES

"Even the truce between the two legions didn't last long. The day came when both legions tried to take control of the piece. Watching this, a part of Eternal's spirit which is in the form of a blade rune created a spell over itself such that only a worthy successor could only attain it. Each legion selected a King and Queen, respectively, and they formed a truce again. The King of stickers and Queen of space dragons. They began a tournament began to find that worthy successor. Though there were still some factions within the two legions who didn't like the idea of the tournament and wanted the piece for themselves as it held untold powers."

"The blade could make one invincible. The Queen of the space dragons had a secret evil plan to claim the piece for herself and rule the planet. She had convinced many stickers and space dragons to join her side. But she never showed any bad side as she wanted it to be a secret till the successor was chosen. The Queen can't be trusted. The girl who brought you here, the one who was caressing Leo, she is the daughter of the Queen, and the boy is the son of the King. The King seems to be a just person."

"So that's how everything is. Now I have told you all I know. Lady, who are you? Why are you both here?"

Rose: "Ah, I am sorry. My name is Rose. I am a Cloudscar, and I live on Ranxus. This is Leo, the rightful heir to Ranxus and also the Wingblade. We came here to get the piece of Eternal."

Dr Hari: "Ah, so it really is you, Lady Rose. It's a pleasure to meet you. I have heard stories about you from my childhood. So, this is Leo, the prophesized child. If you are going to get the piece, you have to be very careful. The Queen is looking for the chance to steal it. You might need all the help you can get. I suggest you get people on your side by the time tournament ends. No one knows what kind of rounds will happen until they are announced."

"There might be one person who can help you get people on your side. He is trusted by everyone. He is said to be a Cloudscar, though I don't recall his name. He was captured recently, just three weeks before you. Maybe you should talk to him."

Rose and Leo looked at each other and then looked at him again.

Rose: "A Cloudscar? Hmm. It sounds like someone we might know. Yes, we will meet him and talk to him. What about you? Won't you be participating in the tournament?"

Dr Hari: “No, I won't. I will be at the Queen's side, watching the tournament as I have to operate on the dead bodies using the blood of the Queen. You see, Queen is trying to spawn hybrids who can obey her command at will and are immortal. She wants to form a hybrid army on this planet. She keeps pushing me. If I refuse, she will torture me in the worst possible way. She won't even allow me to die. I have no other choice.”

Leo: “Hybrids?”

Dr Hari: “Yes. I have experimented on many, but all came out as failure and were caged deep underground. Also, I have heard rumours that recently, a Cloudscar has sided with the Queen to get the piece of Eternal. No one knows who it is or whether the rumour is true or not. Just be careful. Come sleep for now. You are going to need it. Soon it will be time. Good night.”

Rose and Leo nodded and wished him back good night and slept off. They knew it had become way too dangerous, and to get out of it, they had to win the tournament somehow. But the question was how. They had decided to meet up with the captured Cloudscar and talk with him. After a long night, the morning dawned. It was the day of the tournament. All of them were shaken up by those girls who had brought Leo and Rose. The girl who forcibly kissed Leo winked at him when she saw him, at which Rose gave an angry gaze towards the girl and Leo.

Watching this, the other five humans shivered and didn't say anything. They were all taken to a big wall with a normal wooden gate in the middle, and four humans, Rose and Leo, were pushed inside and the doors locked from the outside. The doctor was taken to the Queen. They looked around and saw other beings of various other races. It was a ring of a wall that covered a huge area. There were lots of beings in that ring. Seemed around 100. Rose and Leo searched for the Cloudscar, hoping to see a familiar face, but they didn't get the time to scan properly. The ground started moving beneath their feet.

Everyone was separated by walls of giant stones. It was a maze that was made up of stones. Hardly the maze has formed, a voice echoed. It was the queen. She explained the rules of the first round. The Queen spoke in a loud voice:

"Welcome to the Legion Tournament. Each of you was brought here to participate in it so that we can find a worthy successor who can inherit the piece of Eternal. The piece will show up only to the being who is worthy. If you win the tournament, not only do you get the piece, you are free and can go back to your home. Let the tournament begin."

"The first round is revolving blades. Each section of the maze has been assigned to the player. There is a key that can open the lock to the path to the center of the maze. If you reach the center, you will win. There are 50 keys in total. The maze will change every second when the round begins, and revolving blades will be thrown at you from random directions. If you come across an opponent, you will have to fight each other while avoiding the blades and getting the key. The keys have been placed at random. Find the keys and reach the safe zone. Let the round begin."

No sooner had she spoken the last line; the maze started moving. Leo was looking here and there to move but didn't know where to start. Then suddenly, he heard a sound. As he turned around quickly, he saw quite many crisscrossed arc shaped blades revolving towards him in the air. Leo quickly bent down on all fours to avoid them. Leo knew it wouldn't be so easy. The maze kept changing without rest, and Leo had to keep avoiding it every now and then. As he kept avoiding the blades, he saw a key that lay not far from him. But due to revolving blades, it was not easy for him to reach. Just as he decided to go for it, he found another being in sight, looking at the same key. That being was a space dragon.

Leo: "I don't want to fight you. Come with me. Let's go together into the maze."

The man: "You think I am going to believe what you say? The key is mine and mine alone, and if you try to take it, I have no choice but to kill you."

The man spoke with a threatening voice, and Leo knew it was useless to convince him. Seeing no other choice before Leo, he leapt forward towards the key at the same time as his opponent. They had a hard time avoiding the blades and sneaking near to the key. Leo reached the key first and tried to take the key, but the man just knocked his hand out of the way with his clawed foot, in turn, scratching Leo's arm. Leo screamed in pain, but his scream died out among the revolving blades. While Leo was distracted by his arm, the man reached out to take the key, and Leo caught his hand. They got engaged in hand-to-hand combat while avoiding the blades.

It was a risky position to fight in. Leo kept on trying to convince the man while fighting to join him, but he never listened. It went on for a few minutes when all of a sudden, the man lost his balance. The man fell into the path of a couple of revolving blades that were coming towards him. Leo caught his hand and moved him out of the way while Leo's legs and shoulders got grazed from the blades. The man looked at Leo and realized he was really trying to help him. The man swooped down and took the key and handed it over to Leo and spoke:

"You saved my life. You can have this key. Go ahead and find the lock. Save yourself."

Leo: "No, I will save both of us. Come with me."

The man nodded and spoke:

"My name is Joston."

Leo: "My name is Leo."

Leo and Joston started searching for a keyhole together, avoiding the blades. They both split up in the opposite direction to search for it. Just then Joston's voice was heard:

"I found it, Leo. Quick. Come here."

No sooner were the words out his mouth, Leo swiftly moved towards Joston. He was just a foot away from Joston when the wall near him just exploded, and blades with flames flew everywhere. Joston stood in front of Leo and shielded him from the incoming blades. There were too many, and Joston got stabbed with those blades.

Leo: "Nooo. Joston."

Just then, two contenders came in to view who were fighting. One was a drifter, and the other was a sticker. They were both furiously fighting over the key, which flew right into Leo's hand. Joston fell down to the ground and died right after. The other two looked at Leo, and the drifter spoke:

"You there, give me the key. It's mine."

Just then, the sticker butt in and spoke: "No, it's mine."

They both started fighting. Leo shouted for them to stop, and they both looked at Leo.

Leo: "Guys, please hear me out. Help me to save this planet and its people from being destroyed. I can save you all. Let's go through the gate together and win this round. How about that?"

The drifter nodded, but sticker denied and spoke:

"Why should I trust you? You are not from our planet. You don't belong here. Also, if I don't follow the Queen's order and kill the beings in this round as much as I can, my father will be killed by her. It's the same for many other stickers and space dragons taking part in the tournament. If I help you, how do you even suppose I save my father?"

Leo: "Listen, buddy. It's not over. I am the only one here who can hear the voice of the piece of Eternal. I was chosen by Eternal to bring peace, and that I will. I will help you fight the Queen off this planet before she ruins it further, so come with me and help me save everyone. And if I fail, you still can kill me. How about it? Do we have a deal?"

Sticker: "Alright. It's a deal, then. I am Hersit."

Drifter: "I am Prac."

Leo: "I am Leo. Let's go now. Before it gets worse."

Leo stood up and handed over the key to Hersit. Due to the explosion, there were no blades, so they separately walked towards an empty area surrounded by three walls. As soon as the walls detected the key, a lock opened up. Leo inserted the key and turned it into the keyhole and a path opened up. Prac and Leo walked into the entrance. Leo managed to go through the entrance. But as soon as Prac stepped onto the entrance, a laser was set up, which destroyed Prac into pieces. Leo and Hersit were shocked. The walls closed off again.

It seemed only one could enter with the key. Leo clenched his fists in anger. A moment later, the door opened up, and Hersit entered. They both now walked on to the straight pathway, which led them to a circular waiting area where 48 other participants were waiting. Everyone stared at the latecomers. From among the crowd, a voice echoed, which spoke Leo's name and Rose emerged and hugged Leo tightly.

Rose: "I am glad you made it out alive."

Rose and Leo smiled at each other, but their smile died down with a loud sound.

Chapter – 16

LEGIONS TOURNAMENT – KILLER HYBRIDS

The same voice that spoke before the 1st round spoke again:

"Well done, warriors. Time for 2nd round. All you have to do is survive for 1 hour inside the catacombs and not get killed by the killer hybrids. No one is allowed to forfeit. You will be able to choose a weapon each upon entering the catacombs to protect yourself. Let the round begin."

As soon as the voice died down, the floor on which all the beings were standing on, starting going downwards. The space dragons and stickers shuddered as the floor went down while others just wondered as to what was going to happen. Rose quickly took the chance to fill in Leo with something.

Rose: "Leo, I found the Cloudscar that Dr Hari told us to approach to. And look who it turned out to be."

Leo glanced over Rose's shoulder and whom should be walking towards him but none other than Jin himself. He had survived the explosion. Jin came near them and Leo gave him a hug. He was glad seeing Jin again. Finally, they were reunited.

Leo: "What happened to Dan and Von? Where are they?"

Jin took a deep sigh and spoke:

"I am sorry Leo, Dan and Von were captured by Kate, and they are under her captivity now. You need to find the piece and free them and everyone else. Also, Master Taston died as he tried to protect what was left of Ranxus. I am sorry, Leo. It was too late. Rose told me everything, so don't worry, I will help you when we finish this round. Stay close to me, you two. Let's finish this round and talk later."

Rose and Leo nodded. Leo indicated Hersit to stay close too. After quite a while, finally, the floor came to a resting stop. It was an old catacomb. There were old dark caves everywhere. It was a maze in there. Two vaults opened up in opposite directions right near the entrance of the caves. All the beings just rushed to get their hands on the weapons. The weapons were nothing special. They were just the same as what humans used in the old days, like bow and arrow, swords, battle axes, spears, etc. Rose took bow and arrow while Leo and Jin each took swords. Hersit went for the battle axe. All the blades and arrow heads were made of red scales.

Everyone just regrouped into the center, not knowing what to expect. Few tail-enders stayed away from the group, too arrogant to be careful. There was a rustling of feet, and the next moment, a being near one of the caves was slashed into pieces in a blink. No one saw who did it. Whoever did it was fast. Everyone had their gazes on the lookout for the unknown creature. Then all of a sudden, someone screamed.

Everyone looked in her direction. She was pointing at something coming towards them. As everyone averted their gaze upwards, all they saw was a figure dropping on them and bam, the figure dropped right onto that girl and killed her, meanwhile creating a cloud of dust.

Everyone just ran randomly into the caves, too afraid to face them, except Jin, Leo, Rose and Hersit. They moved away from the cloud of dust. A shadow moved among the dust and came closer and closer towards them. Finally, it stepped out of the cloud of dust onto the clear ground. The creature was very creepy to look upon. There were four bodies attached back-to-back, forming a square. Each body had two arms. They had four legs in total. They wore just torn shorts and nothing else. Their eyes were black, and they had fangs protruding from their mouth. They had no nostrils or a nose to breathe. But instead, they had three slits just beneath their big pointy ears.

Their body was covered with stitches. And their body was brown in colour. Each hand held an arc-shaped blade. They had no hair. No eyebrows. And their feet had long claws, and their fingernails were sharp.

Hersit: "We are doomed. These are the Killer Hybrids."

Leo: "Killer who?"

Hersit: "Killer hybrids. For a long time, Dr Hari, a scientist in genetic research, has been experimenting on beings to create hybrids thus, creating these monsters. They were so powerful and tough to kill that they were caged up in these catacombs. They couldn't be controlled by the Queen. I hate the Queen."

Leo: "Calm down, Hersit. We will fight together and win this round."

Slowly and slowly, the killer hybrid crept towards the group, baring its blades and fangs at them. Jin looked at Hersit and asked:

"You there. What is its weakness?"

Hersit: "I am afraid there is only one weakness. You have to stab the heart. Though the problem is you have to stab all the four at once, or you won't be able to kill it. But to stab its heart is a tough call since they have a good defence and offence. They are really tough to handle."

Jin: "That explains a lot. We have no choice. We all attack together. There must be some weak spot we can find. Keep your distance and attack. Just don't get killed. Go."

All four of them sprung at the creature while the creature also dashed towards them. The attack had to come from the four sides. It was the only choice left. Swords clashed; metals clanked. The rushing of feet. It was quite a struggle for them. Trying to find a weak spot seemed impossible no matter what they tried.

Even sneak attacks weren't effective. The continuous battle was getting them tired. Just then Jin found an opening and he jumped into the air and went headlong into their blind spot in the middle of their backs. No sooner had Jin's head reached their waist when each one of their hands showed the blade back into the middle where Jin's head was. For a moment, Jin thought he was a goner. Luckily the blades missed his head.

Jin quickly backed away. Defending their attacks on him. Jin kept on thinking and thinking when suddenly Leo cut off one of the creature's hands and saw it regenerate, but there was a time gap of 3s. It was a small-time gap, but at least they had hit a weak spot finally. Now the question was the timing. They had to time everything exactly at the same time. One mistiming could deal a deadly blow.

Jin blocked his attacker's attack and held his hands with a firm grip, and spoke:

"Guys, I think I have found a weak spot. Listen, we have to do this together at the same time, or it won't mean anything. Cut off their hands all at the same time. There will be a 3s window until they regenerate their hands. In that window, we will stab their hearts. Let's do it. On my mark, just go."

Jin quickly stepped back after pushing the creature's hands away. Others followed the same suite. The creature glared as Jin gave the signal to launch the attack, and together, they attacked the creature. As the creature swung its hands to attack, four of them cut off the creature's hands at the same time, and without losing time, they quickly stabbed the heart. But the 3s window wasn't enough. All four of them received cuts to their body as their arms regrew.

They were not fast enough. But they had succeeded with the strategy and stabbed the hybrid. As four of them stepped away, the hybrid writhed in pain as white blood oozed out of its wounds and fell to the ground. The place where the blood fell, plants grew out of it. However, the plants were small in size, beautiful to look at. Slowly the hybrid died and turned into ash.

Four of them picked up their weapons. Now the main problem was it was only one hybrid down, and there were lots more. Screams were heard throughout the catacombs. As Leo's group had stabbed the hybrid, it had let out a scream calling out for help, and all the other hybrids came rushing towards them. The ground shook with their stampede. Next moment they were surrounded.

Hundreds of those hybrids had appeared and surrounded them. It looked like they had entered hell and were fighting the inhabitants there. It was clear. There was no chance of going out alive. But those four weren't those kinds of people who would give up so easily or go down without a fight. With each breath they took, their firmness on their weapons got tighter. Their intentions were clear. Kill as many as possible.

Rose: "Leo, now would be a good time to bring it out."

Jin looked at Rose and spoke:

"Bring what out? What are you talking about, Rose?"

Rose: "He awakened his powers not long ago. He just needs to remember it to awaken it again. (Seeing the shocked face of Jin, Rose continued:) Don't worry. I will tell you when we get out of here alive. Come on, Leo, try it."

Jin: "Alright, Rose. Be sure to tell me what all happened. Leo, we are waiting."

Leo closed his eyes for a moment and tried to remember that feeling, but suddenly he remembered his mother's dying moment and her face. He quickly opened his eyes and spoke:

"I am sorry, I can't. I see my mother's face when I think about it. It's difficult."

Rose moved to Leo and placed her hands on his shoulders, and spoke:

"Listen, Leo. If you don't turn, we will face the same fate like your mother did. She is not dead, Leo. She is still alive in here. (she touched his heart with one hand). It's alright, Leo. Remember, we are here by your side and will never leave you."

Leo nodded and closed his eyes, but a sound made him open his eyes. The hybrids came dashing towards them. There was no time to think. All four of them got into battle. There were too many of them to handle. Leo's group received cuts everywhere on their body. While fighting, Leo lost his balance and fell. A hybrid just raised its blade to kill him when Rose protected Leo with her body. The blade cut her back, and blood oozed out.

Leo caught Rose and hugged her, crying. She was wounded badly but thankfully not dead yet. Rose raised her hand and touched Leo's cheeks and spoke:

"Leo, ... it's alright.... Everything will be fine."

Saying this, she fainted. Leo was devastated. He didn't want to lose her. No sooner had that thought crossed his mind, he went back to the day he awakened his powers. His desire to protect awakened his powers again. He finally had become a Wingblade again. The only difference was he was calm this time compared to the other time. He was able to stay in touch with his emotions.

He looked at Rose and quickly brought out his hand and cut it with the arrow's tip and dropped his blood onto her wounds. The wound just healed quickly. The hybrids froze in their place so did Jin and Hersit too. Leo gave an aura of a powerful being which made the hybrids shudder. Even the Queen watching it was scared inside but didn't show it on the outside. Watching Leo's awakened side, a figure walked in to view besides the Queen. The figure was none other than Kate herself.

Kate: "So, he has awakened his powers at last. Well, it will be easy now. Get your people in position. Steal the blade as soon as Leo has it. You won't be able to kill him, but you can stall him as your people steal the piece."

The Queen: "I know what I have to do. Don't order me around, woman. (turning to her soldiers) go forth and bring me the piece. Steal it when he gets it. Kill his friends."

The King: "You can't kill them. You have no authority alone to do that. You……."

He couldn't complete the sentence, and the next moment, his head rolled to the ground.

Chapter - 17

LEGIONS TOURNAMENT - FINAL SHOWDOWN

Kate: "There's the nuisance gone. Go ahead."

Scared of what Kate had done to the king, the other beings present there stood frozen at their spot. The soldiers went away towards the arena. Meanwhile,

Inside the catacombs, with Leo awakened, it was clear who was going to win. Leo just waved his nerve blades, and the two nearby hybrids were cut into two pieces along with their heart. Leo waved his blades again, and two more fell. He closed his eyes, and his body was lifted into the air.

Leo: "All of you, get down and stay down till I say it's safe."

All three of them lied down as the remaining hybrids just dashed forwards towards Leo. The space-coloured scales projected the shadow of the scales and formed a circular ring above. The ring started rotating. The next moment, blades similar to those in Leo's hands formed, pointing towards those hybrids. The next moment Leo just waved his hand,

and the blades just swooped down with tremendous speed cutting down all the hybrids around Leo until none of them was left standing. The others who were watching it stood frozen to the spot to the tremendous power display by Leo.

Another set of hybrids appeared on the ground; meanwhile, the hybrids standing at the cave entrances above glared at Leo for killing their brethren but also were scared to jump down and attack him. Leo waved both of his hands, and a gust of wind froze the hybrids in their tracks on the ground. He spoke:

"Don't do it unless you all want to die. Let the warriors go, and we will leave you in peace."

The hybrids gave way for the warriors as they made their way back to where Leo and the group were. They regrouped together, facing the hybrids. The floor on which they stood slowly started rising to the upper ground. Leo still was in his awakened form, so no one dared to attack him as they went up. As soon as they reached the surface, Leo knelt down as he had lost his footing. He was almost exhausted after he reawakened his form. Jin stood up and held up Leo from one side and helped him stand up, and suddenly, someone on the other side held Leo. It was none other than Rose. She had healed up thanks to Leo's blood.

Just then, a light showed up in the sky and a shiny piece of what seemed to be a blade with star shaped runes on it in the form of space colour appeared. It was the piece of Eternal. The piece they had been searching for all these years. It came down slowly in front of Leo, and a voice which came from the piece spoke:

"Hello, Leo. I am part of Eternal herself. I have been waiting for you all this time. I am glad you finally made it here. I could have found you myself earlier, but I decided not to. Not until you were ready. Now you are ready, so take this piece and combine it with other pieces. Then only I can be revived, and Eraser can be stopped."

Leo stretched out his hand and took the blade rune into his own hands. It was kind of hot, but it didn't burn his hand.

"Leo, I need to tell you some……"

She couldn't complete it as they all were surrounded by the enemy soldiers. Rose and Jin let Leo sit down on the ground as he was unable to fight right now, and they both stood protecting Leo. Hersit and all the other warriors too joined in. After all, Leo had saved them from dying. The leader of the army came forward and spoke:

"Give us Leo, and we will let you go. Resist, and you all will die."

He spoke those words with a smirk. It was clear from his smirk whether Leo was handed over or not, they all would be killed. Leo stared into the army and didn't find the daughter of the Queen there. She stayed with the Queen herself. Jin looked at Rose and nodded and spoke loudly:

"I won't hand Leo over to you, and anyone who forcefully tries to take him will have to face me. I will die rather than giving him up."

Every warrior with Leo seemed to agree with Jin. There was no time to waste chatting, and both sides clashed. Everywhere metals clanked. Jin asked the warriors not to kill anyone as they were all just obeying the Queen's command. So, they just kept knocking the enemy unconscious. Jin and the other successfully defeated the army after quite a long battle. Watching her soldiers get defeated, the Queen just smashed down her throne and shouted in anger:

"I will kill him myself and get that piece."

At this, Kate started laughing and spoke:

"Hahaha. Do you think? Your army was useless, so will be you. Look what they did to your army. You won't even stand a chance against them. You will never be able to get better of them."

The Queen: "Who do you think you are, woman? I am the Queen here, the most powerful one. A worm-like you can do nothing to….."

Kate didn't let the Queen complete her sentence and severed her head which rolled to the ground. She had killed her. Seeing her mother getting killed in front of her, her daughter was frozen with fear and couldn't say anything.

Kate: "See how powerless you are. You couldn't even defend yourself. Time for me to enter the arena. (turning to the two Assyclops and her space dragon) let's go."

The space dragon turned into his dragon form, and Kate and Assyclops got on him and rode towards Leo, destroying the arc in the process. The piece of Eternal felt Eraser's presence which crept up at a fast speed. She spoke:

"Leo, Kate is here. Though she is not the sister, you once knew but possessed by Eraser now. You need to do as I tell you, or she will take the piece. You need to stab yourself with me. Do it quickly now. Trust me."

Leo knew there was no time to waste, especially since Kate was coming. He quickly took the blade rune and stabbed his chest with it just as when Kate came in to view. Kate screamed in anger as she saw Leo stabbing himself.

Kate: "Nooo. That piece belongs to me. How dare you?"

Kate was furious. However, it wasn't the real Kate, Eraser herself, who was saying things and making her do things. As soon as Leo stabbed himself with the blade rune, it entered inside him. The stab had sent a shockwave that threw off everyone to the ground away from Leo and erected a barrier around everyone else except Leo. Kate, her dragon and the Assyclops landed near Leo. Leo's eyes became space coloured. Leo had absorbed the power of the piece. It now flowed inside him.

Eternal's soul: "Hello Eraser, we finally meet again. It's been a while. You seem to be in great shape. Leave Kate at once and go back. You don't belong here."

Eraser's energy: "Neither do you. Join me. Let's rule this universe together and teach these people a lesson who dare to mess with nature itself. As a consideration, I will let these beings live. How about it?"

Eternal's soul: "You think I would believe what you said? I know very well how double-crossing you can be. I guess talking is useless."

Eraser's energy: "Bring it on, sister."

Eternal's soul: "Leo, let me handle it this time."

Eternal's soul took over Leo's body. Blades came out of his hands. On the blades were space-coloured lines helically shaped right in the middle from top to bottom of the blade. It was moving in the helical structure as if it were blood. A thin layer of black energy was engulfing Leo's body like armour. Kate also had blades in her hand and of the same manner as Leo's but engulfed in silver energy. The next moment both of their blades clashed. Those blades were born of the same core. Each time those blades clashed, the sky sparkled with lightning and clouds formed. Meteors started falling from the skies to the ground, destroying the arcs and the rocks.

Meteors also fell on the warriors, but they were unharmed due to the barriers. The battle was so intense that no one could move. A meteor fell onto Eternal and Eraser too. Eraser destroyed it with her blades. Seizing the moment, Eternal just knocked away the blades from Eraser's hands. Flares made of space colour came out of Eternal's back and pinned Eraser to the ground. Eternal raised her blades to stab Eraser when Leo stopped Eternal from doing that.

Leo: "No Eternal. Please don't. She is my sis no matter what. Please don't kill her."

Eternal: "Leo, this isn't the moment to have pity. It's the only way. Do it now before it goes wro…."

Seizing the moment when Eternal froze, Eraser just stabbed Leo's body with her right hand. She started drawing Eternal's power into herself. Leo woke up and kicked Eraser just in time and prevented her from taking Eternal's power completely. With some of Eternal's power taken inside her, Eraser knelt on the ground as she felt the surge inside her body. She smiled. Suddenly there was a movement as the dragon took its shape again, and Kate and the Assyclops got on its back and flew towards the portal quickly.

As Eraser took a part of Eternal's energy from Leo's body, the barrier too dissipated. Leo knelt as he had become completely exhausted. Rose, as well as the Queen's daughter, came running straight to help Leo. Jin and Hersit also rushed to Leo's side. Rose gave a scornful look at the girl, but she didn't want to push since time was of no essence.

Jin: "What do we do now? Kate would probably go to the portal and seal it up to trap us here. If we don't get out, who knows what she will do on earth."

Leo: "Let's go to the portal. There is no time to lose."

Leo tried to walk but fell down.

Rose: "Leo, you are not in the condition to go. But if you insist on going, then I will carry you on my back."

Rose knelt and offered Leo to carry on her back when the girl stopped her. She spoke:

"I am Mijei, a space dragon. On this day, I swear on my life to follow you, Leo, till the end."

She changed herself to a space dragon and asked her to climb on. She indicated other space dragons to help everyone. Watching her, everyone followed her suit. They knew it was time to fight back and go back to their rightful place. Even the space dragons that were present there, hated Eraser for destroying what was left of their homes. All of them flew towards the portal. Kate had reached the portal and was about to enter it when she turned to see Leo and everyone else catching up to her. Kate looked at her space dragon, and he nodded as he took the flight.

With a single wave of his wings, he sent a gust of wind, knocking down everyone to the ground. He was very powerful. Kate and others got into the portal quickly. As soon as they had reached the other side, Kate released silver energy from her hand, which started breaking the portal apart. Seeing the portal falling apart, Leo knew there was no time to be lost. He spoke:

"Mijei, use your full strength to throw Jin and Rose into the portal. I don't have the strength to go, so I will rest here for now and gather my strength, and also, I need to talk with Eternal too."

Jin looked at Leo and spoke:

"No, Leo. We cannot leave you behind."

Leo: "You both have to leave for now and make sure you slow down Kate and rally all the forces you can get. I will join you all soon. Right now, we need to stop her. You two need to hold the ground until I get there, please. Trust me."

Jin and Rose knew Leo was right. Rose let Leo down to the ground. She hugged him and kissed his lips and got up. She walked to the tail of the dragon along with Jin. As Jin was getting on to the tail, Rose looked back at Leo and spoke:

"Come back soon. I will be waiting."

Leo nodded as Rose turned around and got on to the tail too. Mijei pushed her tail back and swung both of them at tremendous speed into the portal. As soon as they disappeared into the portal, it was completely destroyed.

Chapter - 18

ONE LAST STAND

As Kate destroyed the loophole, there was a loud explosion that sent debris everywhere. The space dragon shielded her with his wings. Due to the explosion, Kate or Eraser didn't notice when Jin and Rose flew past them at high speed. Now with the loophole destroyed, Leo was stuck on another planet, and there was no one else to stand up to her. But she knew it wouldn't be long before Leo turned up again. So, there was no time to lose.

She sent Assyclops away with a letter to their new chief while Kate flew back to her kingdom to set her plan in motion. She landed on the marble ring and there was Gare waiting for her along with a couple of other Xerkers. Gare was the commander of Xerkers.

Kate: "Bring those three here."

Dan, Von and Viola were brought before here. They were dressed up in the clothes they wore on the ceremony day. They had bruises on them and blood droplets on their clothes. Kate smirked at them and spoke:

"Hope my fellow Xerkers have shown you proper hospitality."

Viola: "Just kill us. Why keep us alive?"

Kate: "Oh no-no. I will kill you slowly as you see and suffer watching others die around you. I will let you know that Leo won't be coming to help anymore. He is stuck on another planet. He was exhausted when I left. Haha, probably dead by now. Your hope is dead. Soon will be this planet and with it you all. I will make you a deal. If you serve me, I will spare your life."

Viola: "Never. Get lost. Leo is alive, and he will come to save us."

The other two nodded while Kate laughed. She spoke:

"Well, well, well. I commend your belief. Let's see who wins. You will witness the end yourself. Take them away and hitch them to the spikes. Gare, stay here. I need to speak with you. Rest all of you can leave."

Kate talked with Gare for long before he left Kate alone. Then Kate sat down and closed her eyes to concentrate on Eternal's power inside her. Meanwhile, somewhere down the African coast, Jin and Rose fell into the ocean shore. Since it was water and sand, they didn't get hurt much. They both got up completely wet and covered in sand.

Rose: "That girl. I will seriously beat her up. She planned this, didn't she?"

Jin: "Come on, Rose. You know that's not true. She only threw us with such a force so that Kate wouldn't notice while she was destroying the portal."

Rose: "Alright, alright. Now, what do we do?"

Jin: "We will do what Leo wanted us to do. Buy him time as much as we can. I will go west, and you go east. Let's rally as many troops as we can and meet up in Asia. In case I will send two spies to keep watch on the activities of Kate just in case. I am sure Leo will come."

Rose: "Alright."

They both departed in opposite directions. Meanwhile, on the planet of four legions, Leo was resting on the bed inside the arc in deep sleep as Mijei caressed his hair gently. What seemed to be like a deep sleep wasn't an actual one. Leo was in a deep trance. He was standing inside a space structured room. A figure popped up out of nowhere. He quickly went into fight mode. She was space coloured completely, but her body was covered with a thin layer of dark matter. She had normal eyes and mouth. She spoke:

"Hello, Leo. No need to be alarmed. I am just the part of energy of Eternal."

Leo: "So, is this how Eternal looks like?"

Eternal's soul: "No Leo. My actual appearance is different. I am just the soul's energy here. Listen, I need to tell you a couple of things."

"I am sorry you have to go through these problems. Leo, you shouldn't have stopped me when I tried to kill Kate. All this would have been over if I had killed her. All of this could end."

Leo: "No, Eternal, I can't let you kill her. She is my only sister. I know I can save her with your help, but you have to guide me."

Eternal's soul: "Leo, there is no other way. You have to stab her with my energy. Whether she dies or not, it's all up to her. She can make a choice. Time is running out, and this is the final battle. Kate will go all out here. Listen to what I am about to tell you. It's important."

"Since she was just able to take a small part of my power from you, it will take four days to combine Ranxus and Ruzone together. That is combining both the energies together. The moment she combines the energies together, you must stab her with my energy and further stab the combined energy ball along with Kate and smash it into the surface of the planet with full force."

Leo: "Wait, what? Are you trying to kill my sister and others as well? I won't go according to your plan at all then."

Eternal's soul: "Wait, Leo. Let me finish first."

"After you smash the energies with core, there will be a massive explosion. During which you have to use a time warp spell and trap the beings of the planet inside the time warp."

Leo: "How do I trap them inside?"

Eternal's soul: "You have to convert their living energy into soul energy and trap them in there. Meanwhile, I will try to save what will be left of the planet. Though I cannot guarantee I can save anything at all. So as a safety measure, the moment you trap them, I will transfer some of my energy to the time warp just in case I need to get them safe on another planet."

Leo: "What about me?"

Eternal's soul slowly heaved a deep sigh and spoke:

"Alas, even I don't know what will happen to you. Will you die or will you lose your memories, or will anything else happen to you. It's a mystery. But no matter what happens, it will not be a waste if you save all those beings. The fate of the planet cannot be changed, but the fate of the beings living on it can be changed."

Leo: "Ok. I will do anything to save them."

Eternal's soul: "We have four days at most. I am sorry, Leo. There's no other way right now."

Leo: "It's alright. If anything happens to me, please look after those people for me, especially Rose and Jin."

Eternal's soul: "I will. And Leo, I will do everything in my power to save you. Since my whole body isn't here, I can't exert my full power right now. Rest and recover. You need to start your journey on the third day."

Leo: "Ok, I got it."

Leo suddenly opened his eyes and slowly sat up. He seemed calm and clear. He looked around and realized he was inside the arc and Mijei was right there sitting with her head resting on the bedside. She had dozed off while nursing Leo. Leo softly got out of bed and walked outside without making a sound. As soon as Leo stepped outside, he saw the beings and the warriors gathering up stockpiles of resources.

Leo looked at the sky, wondering if he could do everything right. He felt he was standing in a faraway place from Rose where she couldn't reach him. He was lost in thought that he didn't notice Mijei reach him. Leo stepped back a little after seeing her.

Mijei: "Leo, I am sorry for what happened at that time. Please forgive me."

Leo: "It's alright. I forgive you."

Mijei: "What are you going to do now?"

Leo: "I need to rest up first and gather up my strength. Then, I will go back and fight back to save everyone. Will you and others join me?"

Mijei: "I don't know about others. But I will."

Leo: "Gather everyone, please. I need to speak to them."

Mijei walked away and asked everyone to gather up near Leo. Everyone, including the warriors, made their way to where he was. The whole area around Leo was packed.

Leo: "Listen, everyone, my name is Leo, also called the Wingblade. I need your help to fight back and protect the beings on earth. Will you all give me a hand?"

The warriors who participated with Leo agreed to help, while others just didn't show any sign of helping. One of them spoke up:

"Why should we help you? We are free now, and we can live here in peace. We already lost too many of our brethren. We don't want to lose anyone anymore."

Leo: "You are right. You have lost many. But if you don't help stop Eraser, after she destroys our planet, she won't rest. She might target you all too if you want to live, come and fight with me. I will give you a place to stay and peace to enjoy. What do you all say?"

Everyone seemed to be convinced by what Leo said as they had experienced Eraser's power first hand. Soon it was agreed to go to earth, and the plan was to fly using the space dragons there since the portal was destroyed. They had two days to gather up their strength and armour and weapons. Leo left them and walked to a secluded area to rest and gather up his power. He also wanted to learn how to use Eternal's power better.

Meanwhile, at the marble ring,

Kate was addressing all the Xerkers, which included the prisoners she had taken from two kingdoms as well as the two cities who had fallen under her control. Right beside her was Terra, all chained up to a Xeton rod. The rod was space coloured with blue-coloured lines spiralled on the rod. While Viola, Dan and Von were chained to wooden stakes mounted on a steel cart. She spoke:

"My fellow brethren, the time has come for this planet to fall. Today we start the countdown. We will make our stand at the border of what used to be Russia. There we will combine the cores and destroy the planet. Hail to Eraser. Let's rule the universe."

Everyone exclaimed: "Long live, Eraser. Long live the Queen."

Chapter – 19

TOTAL DECIMATION

Part – I

Kate turned towards Garv, who was standing beside her, and spoke:

"Take everyone towards the border. We will make our stand there. I am going there first. The enemy will be coming soon. Be on your guard. Let's go."

Kate flew on her space dragon as her army followed on foot. Assyclops and space dragons who had taken her side were also there. This was the march to the final fight. On the other hand, Leo had gathered up his strength completely and had somehow been able to handle Eternal's power. Though the power was only little, still, it was dangerous.

Meanwhile, Kate flew over the debris swiftly and finally landed on the border of Russia and Europe. She got down off the dragon, and the dragon turned back himself into his human form and stepped aside. She threw the Xeton rod onto the ground on which Terra was tied up. She wanted Terra to witness everything herself and feel the agony.

Kate closed her eyes, and wings appeared on her back with the nexus blades appearing in her hand. Those blades were the same that appeared in Leo's hands earlier. She flew up into the sky and touched the tip of the hilt of the blade against each other. An ear wrenching sound came out of both blades towards each energy ball. The balls started moving towards each other. The sound was heard all over the planet.

Jin and Rose at once knew that it had started. They had very little time. They had to prepare as fast as they could. Meanwhile, on the planet of the four legions,

Leo was beginning to get used to Eternal's power. For two straight days, he practiced with the newfound power. Slowly and slowly, the power of Eternal merged with his power. He only took breaks for food and sleep. Finally, the day came when they had to leave. Eternal's soul spoke to Leo as he arrived at the place where everyone was waiting:

"Leo, we need to do one last thing before we leave. Do as I tell you."

Leo: "Everyone, stay where you are. Don't move."

Mijei: "What's going on, Leo?"

Leo: "I will explain later."

The next moment he transformed into his Wingblade form, and the blade came out of his hand. Four space-coloured claws like thin rods came out of the upper hand and from the wrist on each arm, forming a shape of rugby football with a gap at the end. In the end, a slender long katana shaped sword formed. But this time, the swords had changed. Both swords had space coloured line in the center extending from beginning till the end of the sword on both sides. The rest of the sword was blue coloured.

Leo struck those swords into the ground, and an electric surge went into the ground. He got up, and the swords retreated into his hand. Mijei came near and asked:

"What was that all about?"

Leo: "Eternal wanted to purify the hybrids before we left. So, she did it with that electric surge. The electric surge will neutralize the genes that made them go berserk in the first place and return them to their original state. It will take time. But by the time you all reach back, they will be fine. Let's go now. No time to waste."

Mijei nodded and turned into a space dragon. Leo got on the top of the dragon, and as soon as he stood in the middle of the hexagonal ring. The space-coloured scales emitted ropes in the form of space-coloured flares and wrapped around his waist. His feet sank knee-deep into the dragon's back, and the dragon just flew away. The others followed the same suite. As soon as Mijei got into space, Leo completely sank inside the hexagonal ring into her belly, and the dragon just flew away towards the nearby wormhole.

Since Leo couldn't breathe in the space, so the dragon was protecting him inside her belly. The same was happening with others too. Wormhole to wormhole, they flew with tremendous speed, this time with no camaflouge as it would be useless since Eraser knew they were coming. It was a long way ahead. But the dragon's speed seemed to make it way less. Leo could see outside from the dragon's belly.

His eyes were amazed by the beauty outside. The millions of galaxies with stars, planets and other heavenly bodies. Meanwhile, somewhere in Asia,

Jin and Rose had met up with their respective armies. It was time for the counter-attack. Compared to Xerkers, their number was a small one. Just then, the scouts sent by Jin to track Kate's movements came back. One of the scouts stepped forward and spoke:

"Master, Lady Kate is at the border of Russia. They are lying in wait. They know we are coming. Lady Viola, Master Dan and Master Von are there with the Xerkers as prisoners. They have been chained to spikes. Terra is also with Lady Kate. She is right beside Lady Kate guarded by two Assyclops."

Jin: "Thank you. (turning to Rose) it looks like it's going to be a hell of a fight. I hope Leo makes it back in time."

Jin continued:

"Let's go now. We can't stand here with Kate right on the top."

Jin and Rose led their armies towards the border. As they neared the border, they saw Kate standing right in front of them with Xerkers behind her, ready to attack any moment. As they reached near them, Kate spoke:

"Good of you two to show up. But nothing can change now. Your numbers are way too less, and we won't spare anyone. You all still have time. Join me, and I will spare all the pain and give you a quick, painless death."

Jin: "Like in hell."

Kate: "Hahaha. How pathetic. No one can help you, no---"

Kate's smile drained off as she averted her eyes to the sky. Watching her, everyone else averted their eyes to the skies. Balls of fire were raining down towards the ground at high speed. They had no time to move out of the way. The balls stuck the ground with a massive force sending dust flying everywhere. As the dust cleared out slowly, Leo and Mijei stepped out along with rest of their group.

Jin: "Finally. You are late, though. But glad you are here."

Leo: "Couldn't be helped. Needed to recover and also Eternal and I had the last thing to do on that planet."

Watching this, Kate laughed and spoke:

"Keh. Cozy up as much as you want. In the end, you will all die. Kneel before me, Leo and I will give you a quick, painless death. Or you can die slowly watching your friends and loved ones die first."

Leo looked up at Kate and spoke:

"Leave my sis right now, and I will spare your life."

Kate: "As if I will."

Kate came down, but Terra remained in the air near the blades while being guarded by the Assyclops. Leo knew that even if he asked her to let them go, she wouldn't listen. Silver blades appeared in Kate's hands as she dashed towards Leo, followed by the Xerkers. At the same time, few remained to guard the prisoners. Leo transformed, and the blades came out of his hand, and he dashed forward, followed by Jin, Rose and Mijei and the rest of the army.

Leo and his comrades were all tensed as they dashed forward towards Kate and Xerkers. The outcome of this war would be catastrophic. It was do or die situation. Kate and Leo just flew at each other, and their blades clashed. As soon as their blades clashed, a gust of wind sent nearby debris flying into the incoming army. Many Xerkers were knocked dead while Rose raised a shield protecting everyone.

The drifters enclosed their hands together in horizontal direction and the shield that was on their clothes, appeared in front of them. From those shields, the three snakes leapt forward towards the incoming Xerkers. The snakes were made of bones in a circular manner and it rotated and created a path forward by pushing them sideways. Then they released their hands and pulled the snake in the middle of the shield bringing out a snake sword. The snake sword had circular bone structure and the bones opened up to grab those Xerkers inside and crush them. The Xerkers in turn brought out the same blades that Kate had and fought back against the Drifters. Others followed the same suite.

Meanwhile, Leo and Kate crossed their blades again and again. Each time their blades clanked against each other; they kept on leaping up into the sky. He found an opening and was about to kick when he stopped. He was still hesitating to hurt Kate. Seizing the opportunity, she kicked him into the ground hard. Leo was hurled way hard into the ground, which sent the nearby debris raining down on him. The next moment, Kate raised one blade, and fire meteors started falling from the skies. As the meteors fell, black clouds formed in the sky, which made the atmosphere heat up tremendously.

The meteors rained down onto the army fighting below. That day lot of beings died. The planet Earth was lit on fire. As the atmosphere heated up, the radioactive dust became active thus creating an electrical surge that created lightning. The armies of both sides were fighting hard. The lightning started striking down and creating ruckus among the fighters. Each time the lightning struck on the ground's surface, there was an explosion.

The next moment where Leo lay, there was an explosion. He emerged from the cloud of dust formed due to the explosion. He was surrounded by the wings at random points, which came out of the rings on his pants. The wings had protected him, forming a shield. As Leo leapt into the air, Eternal's voice echoed in his head which spoke:

"Leo, stop hesitating. You can't protect anyone at this rate."

Leo knew Eternal was right. The scales formed a shadow again and showered blades onto the incoming meteors, destroying them completely. Kate again launched herself at him. In every attack by Kate, it was clear she was trying to kill Leo. Though it wasn't Kate doing that Eraser was making her do. Jin saw Leo was in trouble and tried to help him.

Eight types of two circular rings made of clouds, crisscrossed with each other at its diameter, appeared around Jin in a circular formation. As the pair of circular rings revolved around each other at its diameter, with a shining circular blade forming around the circumference of the rings. The rings just slashed around at the Xerkers that came to attack Leo. Just then, his attacks were stopped by four Xerkers. They were using a sword made out of the silver energy of Eraser. Jin again threw those rings back at those Xerkers, but they stopped it using their sword again and threw it right back at Jin, who had to stop the rings using a shield. The rings disappeared, and as soon as the shield came down, the four Xerkers just threw arc crones at Jin. It was too late for Jin to bring out the shield just when he had removed it.

He tried to shield himself with his hands. The next, there was a loud screaming sound. As Jin opened his eyes, the arc crones were gone, and Xerkers lay on the ground with holes in their bodies and blood flowing out of them.

Chapter – 20

TOTAL DECIMATION

Part – II

Jin turned around to look who was the one who saved his life and who did he find, but none other than Rose herself. On top of both of her hands was a hexagonal plate which was divided into four equal halves, and a circular space coloured line was continuously revolving over the crisscrossed lines rapidly. As the circle kept revolving around at its circumference, six hexagonal blades, which were themselves in the hexagonal structure, were rotating with speed. She looked at Jin and asked:

"You good?"

Jin: "Yeah, thanks to you."

Rose: "Haha. Never saw you get so careless before."

Jin: "Happens."

As soon as Jin finished speaking, they were surrounded again. Soon they both again got busy fighting. Not a long distance away from them was Mijei fighting along with Hersit. They both were giving a tough fight though both of them received wounds too. As the battle prolonged, the ground on which they stood became a river of blood and flesh pieces everywhere. Up in the sky, there was a storm brewing as Kate and Leo fought fiercely, each trying to gain the upper hand on each other. Again, they interlocked their blades which gave Kate an opening, and she kicked him hard and sent him flying into the Xerkers fighting below, in turn killing a few of her own.

She seized this opportunity and pressed together with her hands as if to clap. At once, the clouds cleared, and it was a clear sky with stars visible. The sudden change of the surrounding made everyone stop fighting as they all looked up. Leo, who had fallen on the ground, stood up and looked up at the sky as he dusted off his hands. What happened next froze him and everyone else to the spot. Kate had summoned all of the planets that existed in the solar system onto the earth. Mercury was the hottest, so it destroyed Venus as they both crashed with each other. On the other hand, Saturn destroyed Jupiter due to its rings. In total, four planets were crashing down onto the earth while the planets that had been destroyed were falling down like meteors on earth.

Leo couldn't move because of fear. Sensing this, Eternal took over Leo, and she leapt into the sky. She clanked the hilt of the blades with each other and formed a net. She then sent it flying towards the falling planets and meteors. Though the planets and meteors were destroyed, they were broken into tiny pieces which still fell to the earth and still destroyed the ground a lot, and many were killed.

Kate had been waiting for Eternal to do that, and she closed her eyes and whispered the words:

"Leanaehe celesterina soulica"

It meant awaken celestial spirits. Eternal who heard those words knew at once that she had made a grave mistake in destroying those planets and fallen into Eraser's trap. There was a gas seeping sound. Eternal slowly eased her control over Leo, and as he recovered and recollected as to what happened, he averted his gaze onto the ground while being in mid-air. There was gas forming on four spots. Inside the gas, a spirit formed on the four spots. One spirit was in flames. Another was made of red rocks, another made of ice, and the fourth had two rings in her hand. Eternal spoke in Leo's mind:

"Those are the spirits of the planets I just destroyed—the spirits of Mercury, Mars, Saturn and Neptune. I am sorry, Leo, I didn't realize it was a trap. You cannot defeat those spirits, but you can stop them if you defeat Kate. Please, the time has come for you to rise up and end it."

Leo: "I got no other choice, do I? Is there any way I could save sis?"

Eternal's soul: "Yes, there is. You need to use my power to stab Kate into the planet's core's energy when they combine together and then smash her along with energies into the core. When you do, I will remove Eraser's power from Kate and free her. That's the only way. And it's almost time too. The energies are almost on the way to combine together."

Leo looked behind him, just in time to see the energies had almost reached close to each other. Half a day had passed since the battle began. Leo couldn't believe it. He looked around and saw Jin, Rose, Mijei and Hersit together standing just below where he was. He flew down towards them and landed down.

Rose: "Leo, what do we do now? This has turned to worse."

Leo: "There is a way, but I need all your help. I can't do this alone. Jin and Hersit, you both head towards Viola, Dan and Van and free them while, Mijei, me and Rose will go and free Terra. We need as much help we can get right now."

Mijei: "That's good, but what about those four spirits? Who are they?"

Leo: "Those are the spirits of the planets Eternal just destroyed. Mercury, Mars, Saturn and Neptune. As for handling them, Eternal if you may please."

Eternal's soul: "Leave it to me, Leo."

Leo closed his eyes, and four clones of himself formed. They each had been given a part of Eternal's power. This put a lot of strain on the original Leo himself. Leo spoke:

"Ok now, listen. My clones will keep these spirits busy, but all they can buy are 5 minutes. Within 5 minutes, we need to free them. Jin and Hersit go for Viola, Dan and Von. Meanwhile, Rose and Mijei will go for Terra while I distract

Kate. Once you free them, get out of there. Leave the rest to me. On my mark."

As soon as the clones split up and dashed towards the spirits, Leo spoke:

"Go."

At once, five of them split up. Jin and Hersit raced across the ongoing fighters and made it up to the place where Viola, Dan and Von were. All three of them were wounded badly, but still, they were conscious. Watching Jin, all three of them smiled a little. As Jin and Hersit approached them, four Xerkers blocked their path. They seemed no ordinary Xerkers. They emitted an aura of being the generals of Kate's army.

Jin and Hersit knew it would be a tough fight, but they had to make it quick. Jin quickly launched the rings again, but they were blocked yet again by those Xerkers. Hersit used his blood to form sticking tissues that stuck to the body of one of the Xerker but did no damage. Instead, the Xerkers cut off the tissue. Jin had a sudden idea as he watched it. He asked Hersit to do it again, and this time on all four of them. Hersit used his sticking tissue again, holding those Xerkers to the spot.

Jin knew there wasn't much time, so he quickly used the rings to kill them and freed the prisoners. They took the three behind a nearby boulder and laid them to rest there. Jin asked Hersit to watch over them as Jin took a peek towards the spirits and at the rest of the group who went to rescue Terra. The spirits were still busy fighting the clones. Meanwhile,

Leo once again reached in front of Kate and spoke:

"Eraser, this is your last chance. Leave my sis and all these beings alone and leave. If you don't, I will have to force you."

Kate: "Haha. I would like to see you try that. Give me Eternal's piece, and I will let you live. If you don't, I will take it after I kill everyone."

Leo: "Looks like, it's do or die situation."

Leo once again launched an attack on Kate, but his attacks were weaker as he had used too much energy by creating clones. But he had to distract her for now. Kate responded to his attacks by attacking him back. Slowly Leo led Kate away from Terra and the Assyclops. This gave Rose and Mijei a chance to sneak towards Terra. Now they had to take care of the Assyclops. But it didn't take long for the Assyclops to notice them. They swung the skulled blades at Rose and Mijei, creating a pulse, and blocked them.

But this did not stop Rose. She used the hexagonal blades to split up and fly towards the Assyclops from different directions. The Assyclops use the blade again to shatter those blades into pieces. Rose was devastated with one of her weapons destroyed. She only had the last weapon left. Conjuring another one would take some time, and it was not possible now. Her hesitation for a moment gave Assyclops a moment to attack, and one of the Assyclops raised his blade towards Rose and had almost touched her body when Mijei launched herself between Rose and the blade pushing Rose out of the way.

Another ear wrenching pulse and Mijei's internal body had shattered. She spat out blood and fell onto the ground.

Rose was furious watching it happen. She used the other blade to encircle the Assyclops. She shot out needles towards them. The Assyclops again created a pulse, but the needles just disappeared and re-entered their body inside. As soon as the needles got in, they exploded, releasing nano blades that tore those Assyclops from the inside. She quickly released Terra, and they both went back towards Mijei.

As Rose and Terra landed on the ground near Mijei, they gasped. Mijei was lying down on the ground with blood all around her. Her face had turned pale. Rose knew there was little time left, so she requested Terra to save her life. Terra, in turn, shared her energy with Mijei, which healed up her wounds and repaired her torn down organs and tissues. But couldn't bring back the lost blood. Mijei had barely survived death, but she wasn't in a state to fight anymore.

Jin's group were just a few meters away from Rose but couldn't risk moving right now as they both had wounded on their side. The clones fighting the spirits disappeared. They had made it in time but now was the difficult task. The spirits had begun to move towards Jin's and Rose's group. Leo had to hurry now with no time left. Meanwhile, Leo and Kate were engaged in an intense fight. As soon as the clones disappeared, Eternal's energy returned to Leo, and he knew at once it was time to finish it. Just as the energy had returned, the ground below started shaking violently. The energies had touched each other and began to merge.

The armies were getting tired and weary from all the fighting. They lost their balance as the ground shook violently. The four spirits were killing all those came in their way may it be a foe or a friend.

It created a massive amount of energy which struck down onto the ground in the form of lightning, shaking the ground and destroying it further. Slowly, the energies merged into one. As soon as they became one, there was a huge explosion, and an energy wave sent Leo and Kate flying backwards and cleared the clouds and atmosphere. It was time to finish it. Kate went directly for her blade, which was at the top of the ball of energy, but Leo blocked her.

The scales formed shadows once again on his back, and flares came out of it and grabbed Kate's hands and legs tightly so that she couldn't move. The next moment Leo combined both the blades together and pointed them at Kate. Watching this, the four spirits jumped towards Leo. Leo wasted no time as the blade split into three, and the middle-spaced line plunged forward on its own directly into Kate's chest, pushing her to the energy ball. Leo let go of the flare as Kate couldn't do anything anymore.

Chapter - 21

TOTAL DECIMATION

Part - III

Kate felt herself growing weak because of the blade she was stabbed with and there was no way she couldn't remove it. Leo plunged the blade along with Kate on the top of the energy ball and pinned her. The other two sides of the blade lit up with blue energy while the flares tried to stop the four spirits. The Saturn spirit just threw her rings towards Leo. One ring got shredded to pieces, but the second one was missed, and Leo got stabbed in the back with it. The next moment Rose screamed with shock:

"Nooo, Leo."

Leo mustered up his strength and lifted the energy ball, and quickly smashed it into the ground. The force with which it got smashed was so huge that the ground just broke into pieces and flew in all directions. Everyone lay on the ground to prevent themselves from the incoming debris. Deeper and deeper into the ground, it went until it touched the earth's core. The ground again shook up with huge force. But this time, orange-reddish lights were coming from the ground through the cracks that appeared on the ground.

As more and more the cracks developed and the lights intensified, all the beings that lay down on the ground began to light up in white colour. Leo looked towards Rose and Jin as he spat blood. Tears flowed down Rose's cheeks as Jin and Rose both stared at him. Rose kept yelling out Leo's name. Slowly the beings started to transform into soul energy. They just vanished after transforming into soul energy. Eternal had sent them into deep sleep inside a soul time warp.

Terra disappeared. Leo loosened his grip on the blade and let go of it. He started falling onto the core. More and more cracks went on intensifying. The light showed brighter each time. It was clear that the earth's time was over for now. Suddenly, there was a huge explosion, and the planet split into tiny pieces. The explosion sent a huge wave of energy that split the sun and moon into too many pieces. Everything was gone into ruins. A circular ball made of water and wood was in the center where the planet was as the planet's pieces were still floating around.

Out of the ball emerged Terra, unharmed and safe. Eternal had used her energy to save earth's spirit from being destroyed. However, the spirit looked much like a teenager. It seems like Terra had been reborn. She opened her eyes and looked around at the ball, and spread her arms. She then encircled her hands into a vertical circle. The ball also started reforming and taking a new shape.

With water at the center, the wood started forming into a tree, a big one that rose into space. Four trees grew in four directions, with their roots covering the water ball completely as if protecting it. Leaves grew on the trees, and so did branches. But those branches were normal. They grew bigger and bigger as they extended up to some distance. They were made of both water and wood. The planet's pieces started gathering up at those branches, and slowly large islands formed on those branches.

The islands were vast in the area, with forest covering most of the island. The islands looked just how the earth was when it was formed billions of years ago with just forests, rivers, etc. Earth had been reborn thanks to Eternal. With Eternal's last energy still left inside Terra, she summoned the beings from soul time warp back onto the nearby island. Each island had been wrapped up with a barrier to help the beings on it breathe. Bridges made of wood were formed to connect those islands. The parts of the sun and moon that had been destroyed by the shock wave started to come and get mixed together, forming smaller forms of stars with each star body consisting of half-sun and half-moon. The body was called Semicrone which kept rotating around the islands.

After all the beings were safely summoned back, Eternal's energy inside Terra dissipated. Slowly the beings started to come around as they started coughing and getting up. Terra came down near them. Jin and Rose were also there. Terra walked right up to them. All beings now looked at Terra as she spoke to all of them:

"Citizens of earth, I am Terra, the spirit of the earth. Yes, this planet has been reborn, and I with it, all thanks to

Eternal. I will now appoint two chiefs among you to lead you. Jin and Rose are the new chiefs. They are the best choice. I hope you all agree."

No one seemed to raise any objections. Even the Xerkers had turned back to their original selves as Eternal's energy had purified Eraser's energy inside their bodies. Terra continued:

"Live and prosper. We have been given a second chance. Please don't repeat the same mistake of bringing this planet to the brink of destruction. I will be watching over you all. You have all the resources here. With time everything will be fine. Let's live on. Toward tomorrow."

With this, Terra dismissed everyone. As Terra walked to the edge of the island, she beckoned Jin, Rose, Mijei, Hersit, Viola, Don, and Van to follow her. As they all followed, Rose searched for Leo among the crowd, but he was nowhere to be found.

Rose: "Terra."

Terra: "Yes, Rose?"

Rose: "Where is Leo?"

Terra: "He vanished without a trace. (looking at their worried faces) Don't worry. He is still alive, but I don't know where and I can't pinout his location. The explosion must have thrown him off into a wormhole nearby. I know you all want to go search for him, but you can't leave everyone else. Someone has to stay and look after them."

Rose: "What about Kate?"

Terra: "As for Kate, she too vanished with Leo. So, I am guessing they both fell into the same wormhole. Find Leo first. Who knows, you might find Kate too. (Terra thought for a while and continued) Jin and Viola will remain here and the rest of you will go in search of him. I can't go anywhere as I am tied to the core. I will be going into a deep sleep for a while to recover my powers. Please look after yourselves."

Saying after this, Terra disappeared. The soul time warp seemed to have healed Viola, Dan and Von's injuries too. Even Mijei had recovered. The next moment, four space dragons were summoned. Mijei also transformed into a space dragon. Rose, Dan, Van and Hersit got on top of the space dragons, and only Mijei remained alone with no one on her. Same as Leo, all four of them went into the belly of the dragon as they took off to find Leo. As they took off, Rose glanced at Jin.

Jin: "Find him and bring him back. We are waiting."

Rose nodded as they flew off towards the wormhole.

To be Continued…………………

www.ingramcontent.com/pod-product-compliance
Lightning Source LLC
La Vergne TN
LVHW091324150826
845673LV00006B/1755

* 9 7 9 8 8 9 6 9 9 3 8 0 3 *